W9-AZG-982

The Side Chick Who Turned Into A Wife

-A Novel Written by-

Marques Lewis

Copyright © 2016 by True Glory Publications

Published by True Glory Publications LLC

Join our Mailing list by texting TrueGlory at 95577

Facebook: Marques Lewis

Website: www.iammarqueslewis.com

IG: iammarqueslewis

This novel is a work of fiction. Any resemblances to actual events, real people, living or dead, organizations, establishments or locales are products of the author's imagination. Other names, characters, places, and incidents are used fictitiously.

Cover Design: Michael Horne

Editor: Joy Hammond/Artessa La'shan Michele'

All rights reserved. No part of this book may be used or reproduced in any form or by any means electronic or mechanical, including photocopying, recording or by information storage and retrieval system, without the written permission from the publisher and writer.

Because of the dynamic nature of the Internet, any Web addresses or links contained in this book may have changed since publication, and may no longer be valid. The views expressed in this work are solely those of the author and do not necessarily reflect the views of the publisher and the publisher hereby disclaims any responsibility for them.

1

Acknowledgements

First, I would love to give thanks to God for everything He has done for me. Without Him, I would not be here today, nor would I have written this book. To my parents, Dora and James Lewis, thank you guys for believing in me and being my #1 fans. I love you guys. To my sister, Belinda Frazier-Lewis and brother Greg Lewis, thanks for all the support. To the rest of my family and friends I love all of you guys and thank you for everything. To my fans who have supported me, thank you so much it means a lot to me. I hope you enjoy this book....

Just in case you forgot the name of my books...."The Side Chick Who Turned Into A Wife" Part 1, "Married and Miserable", It's Love For Her" 1, 2, & 3, "The Road To The Perfect Guy" 1, 2, & 3, "Dating Jordan", "How's Your Strippers Dick", "Never Settle Never Again", "The Woman Who Got Away", "Words of Wetness", and "The Man Next Door". You can 1-click or get them on paperback!!!

WITHDRAWN

Welcome To
The Side Chick
Who Turned Into
A
Wife

3 1526 04879904 0

The Side Chick Who Turned Into A Wife

Written By

Marques Lewis

The Prologue

The creaks were loud every time she made a movement lying on the cot. She was cold. The little cotton brown blanket wasn't enough to warm her up. The little small pink TV was on but she looked towards the ceiling. A white envelope slid underneath the cell door and there was a knock. The woman got out of the cot, turned the TV off and picked up the envelope. She sat back down on the cot. She gently caressed her stomach and opened the envelope. It was a letter. She unfolded it and began reading the letter. Tears fell onto the paper as she skimmed through it reading the harsh words. As she continued reading she could hardly compose herself.

"This is my first and last time writing you. I am sending this letter from my job so you won't know where I live at.

I want you to stop writing me. I have taken another job as you can see. Stop sending fucking mail to my other job. I don't want you to continue to keep writing me, because they are sending me letters from there to here. You are going to fuck me up while I am pretty much just getting here. I let you go for a fucking reason. I love my family. You are trying to mess my family up and it won't work. You are a fuckin' slut! I love my wife and you need to know that. There is nothing you can do to make me yours. It is over. We are not together anymore. Hell, to me, we never were. You have to walk away from this.

What we had yeah it was special but now it is over. Goddamn it. I wasn't happy with you. I love my family. You have to accept it and move on.

You are where you are for a reason and you had no reason to attack her. For God's sakes she is pregnant with my child. It is over.

Okay, I don't love you and you will never see me again. It is over. You will be there for a long time because I will make sure my attorney keeps you there. Good-bye bitch!!!! Don't write me back. If you do I will find some type of way to sue you for harassing me. Bitch!"

More tears fell down as she held her forehead. She wished she could repeat that day of violence and not have committed the crime she did.

She crumbled the letter throwing it with force on the floor. She began reading another letter she finished writing him. She didn't care about what he was saying, because she was going to send it to his new job. She loved him and had to let him know exactly how she felt.

"I can sit here and act like I don't miss you. I can act like I don't think about you. I think about you from time to time because the memories we had. I have been here for five months now which seems like ten years. Remember the great sex we had. Don't you remember smiling with me? You were the only air I inhaled. The only man I knew. I wanted to spend the rest of my life with you. I wanted you here in my life with me forever but when you told me it's not going to work it hurt me. I was damn near destroyed.

How could I go on? Everything we had together how could you leave me just like that? You didn't even want to talk about it. Wishing I could rewind history or move myself to where you are now just so we could always be together. You made me change into the wonderful woman I am today and I thank you for that. What happened to us having faith in one another?

What happened to us praying for one another? I sit here as tears come to my eyes on this paper. I can just remember your smile. When I see you smile my whole world lights up. It's hard to let you go because I still love you. I know you came into my life for a reason and it was to change me. You did that. You loved me. You gave me what a man will never give me and that is love.

So I thank you. I wish I could hear your voice one more time. I wish I could hug you that would be heaven to me right now, but all I get is these memories and these disrespectful letters saying "fuck you! You think you are going to enjoy your life and not love me? That bitch who has your heart will never have it like I have it. You are a piece of shit! Do you know that?! Trapped in these four walls being punished for loving you and protecting what is mine. Fuck you Brandon!

Depression, starvation, sleepless nights, stressed out, and lies staying with you. You know what I was weak being with you; I can admit that because all I knew was you. I didn't give a fuck about other men but you. That's it but you repeatedly messed us up.

My love is strong, precious, and only a real man deserve it. Obliviously that wasn't you. What you did to me a couple months ago was unforgiveable. You embarrassed me but you know what I am going to use this time and make myself a better woman.

Just being here is the first step then talking to God and getting to know him better and then finally that will heal my heart. I know you are not mad because I won't leave you alone. Your ass is mad as hell at what I told you. I know my future is ready to treat me right. Brandon, just wait until I get out. Fuck you....you piece of shit!".....

She rubbed her stomach gently and folded the letter to be sent off.

Chapter One

Tell Me What Happened

800x643px size of the room and white walls shaped like pillows boxed her in. The bed sat in the middle of the room with satin white sheets, and a dingy white pillow where she lay he head. The cool air came through the vent. Balled up loose leaf papers cornered each of the four walls as Chelsea stood up with her head first on the concrete gray floor. Her long, black, and straight hair went down to the middle of her back. She wore a white plain long gown with brownish strings to tie herself in comfortably. No shoes on the cool floor as she started to shed a tear. She punched the floor three times. She sat back on her legs and started to look up into the ceiling of white pillows.

"God please make a way. I am so sorry. Please forgive me. I do not deserve to be here anymore. I have learned my lesson God. I have faith that I will be out of here. I know you will make a way God."

There was a knock on the door and she suddenly got up and went against the wall in fear. The door opened and it was an elderly short black woman nurse with curly black hair with grey edges. The light glared off of her burgundy gown and black slippery resistant work shoes. She walked in trying to calm Chelsea down with her hands out.

"Chelsea, it is Nurse Tasha, baby. Everything is fine. I promise. No one is here to give you medicine or make you take your blood pressure," she said stepping slowly towards the room.

There was a white, bald-headed, dark brown eyed, husky male nurse outside waiting with a white straight jacket. Chelsea's breaths were uncontrollable and her eyes dilated.

"Chelsea, please trust me, honey. Everything is going to be fine. She stepped even closer to Chelsea with her hands out showing her she wasn't to mistreat her.

"Tell the other nurse out there with the straight jacket to leave now and don't lie to me and say he isn't there! I know he is!" Chelsea said moving to the other side of the room getting away from Nurse Tasha.

"Now Chelsea, you know I cannot do that. You have to put it on and you know that. It is a part of the policy, so please Chelsea let Mark do his job. It will only take a second."

"No! I am not crazy and I am not dangerous at all."

"Chelsea, you tried to kill someone. How are you not dangerous?!" Nurse Tasha said stomping her feet at her. "Now come put this jacket on. You don't want them to shoot you with that needle now do you?" her voice raised into a country accent.

"Tell him to leave and I will come with you. Nurse Tasha, please understand I made a mistake that day.

Please tell him to leave," Chelsea said moving away from Nurse Tasha quickly with tears forming in her eyes.

Mark stood at 6'4 and 278 pounds, walking in bending his head down with the straight jacket ready for Chelsea.

"Mark, no. If she said she doesn't need it and she is not crazy then I will trust her."

Mark stood there looking at the dumb choice she was making. "Nurse Tasha, are you serious right now?" he said with a deep voice.

She looked at him and looked at the fear in Chelsea's eyes. "Yes, she has been on her best behavior. I trust her. She is just scared of this place that's all. Mark, I have it."

"Are you…"

"Mark please."

Mark turned away slowly and walked off. Nurse Tasha held her hand out for Chelsea to trust her.

"Chelsea, you can trust me. I am here to bring you to your lawyer."

"Where is she?" she asked walking towards her slowly.

She is in the abandoned Crisis room that we use for lawyers when they need to talk to patients.

"Okay, I will go with you." She grabbed Nurse Tasha's hand and they walked out of the door.

They walked down the hallway slowly. The halls were full with nurses. Some were chasing down mental patients and with patients trembling staring at them walking with nurses. Chelsea hated the place and was scared of everyone there.

"Chelsea, let me ask you something why did you do it? I mean I really wanted to ask you ever since you've been here. Why did you do that? You are so much better than that. You had a great job. You were the top of your class, so why did you do that?" Nurse Tasha asked looking at her to the right.

She didn't say anything. "So you do not want to talk to me today? Come on Chelsea, you have only been here for a year. I mean isn't it better than…."

Chelsea stopped and ground her teeth. She turned her head to the left side of her.

"Do not even say it. I have overcome that place and I am glad I did my time. I am here now with only two weeks to go that is what my lawyer is going to say. I know it! All I want to do is go back to my room and think about the days I have left. I know when I go in here and go to my court date everything will be fine."

"Honey, listen, you do understand you tried to kill someone right? You do understand that right?"

"I do understand, okay? I don't need someone to keep telling me about my past. I have done thirty days in jail and a year here now.

I know that God has me and I know what my lawyer is going to say. I am leaving here soon."

"You are one hard headed woman but I hope you are right. That is understandable that you put your trust in

God, because you are supposed to. Well here is the room. She is in there. I will come back to get you once it is over. I hope you get everything cleared."

"Whatever." Chelsea walked inside and Nurse Tasha closed the door.

Her lawyer wore a dark blue suit with a baby blue dress shirt and her dark black flat shoes off by the table. She stood up from the metal bent chair. She was medium built and stood 5'7.

"Chelsea Johnson, it is nice to see you again. Do you remember me, your lawyer Rebecca Williams? We haven't met since the first time you went to jail," she said with a lovely voice showing her pretty white teeth. She pushed her long blonde hair back and kept blinking her baby blue eyes. Her tan white skin reflected off of the cup shape white light.

The room shaped just like Chelsea's room. The squared chandler light swung slowly blinking. The sun shined bright through the little window pane. The room was stuffy.

Chelsea looked at the weather outside. She hasn't been outside over a year.

"Yes, I remember you," she said smiling back looking out the squared glass door. She looked down the hall as far as she could. She glanced at the white and black tile floors.

"Chelsea, I need you to focus honey. We have a lot of important documents to go over. Time is limited so let's start away," Rebecca said slamming her brown briefcase on the table.

Chelsea ignored her and watched the people walking back and forward. She couldn't wait for her release date. She hit her head against the wooden door.

Rebecca instantly reacted, "Oh my God, are you alright? Did you slam your head against the door?"

She didn't say anything. She grabbed her head to press against the pain.

Rebecca cleared her throat. "Listen, Chelsea, I need you to come sit down baby girl, so you can tell me everything that happened that day. Let me go ahead and bring you up to speed. You were denied bond and pleaded not guilty. We also said that your bi-polar disease helped you get a year at the halfway which you are here. Now."

Chelsea smiled because she couldn't wait for her to say she was going to be released soon.

"I need you to tell me everything that happened with you and Mr. Daniels.

Please come sit down", she said standing up pointing at the chair where Chelsea was to sit.

Chelsea turned around and smiled and walked over and sat down. She looked at Rebecca with a creepy twisted grin.

"Ms. Williams, what do you need to know?"

"Please call me Rebecca."

Chelsea not giving a damn what her name was. She just wanted her to inform her when she was getting out.

"You can call me Rebecca, Ms. Johnson, now…"

"If you are not going to call me Mrs. Daniels, you can call me Chelsea."

"But you are not married to Mr. Daniels. Wait you know what," Rebecca smiled knowing that Chelsea was crazy in love with Brandon. "Chelsea, please tell me what happened that day on the airplane. I need to know what happened May 5, 2013."

"Listen, I told you before what happened. Why do I need you to keep telling you what happened when you already know?"

Rebecca slowly took a deep breath getting frustrated. "Listen, what you did was attempted murder on an airline plane. Now you need to understand that jury and the system doesn't play about someone trying to kill someone on an airplane. Now I know what I said when you did thirty days in jail and here at the halfway house that would be good enough, but Chelsea it isn't, because right now you are looking at five years in prison.

Chelsea eyes acted like they were going to pop out of her eyes socket. "What the fuck do you mean five years? I did everything you told me to do."

"If you do not tell me everything that I need to hear you will go away for five. I promise you that is what they are trying to give you right now. If you tell me what

I need to hear then we could get the charges dropped or get you another six months here."

Chelsea jumped up. "That's bullshit and you know it," she said with her shoulders going up and down talking loudly. "You told me that I had to do a year and I was good. What happened?"

"Can you please sit down?"

"What happened?"

"Mrs. Daniels testified against you in court last month. She wasn't going to do it, but she did. They were going to let this thing ride, but she felt that you were a threat to her life. You got one of the toughest judges in Atlanta this time for your case. She wants you locked away. She doesn't even want the money. She just wants you away for a long time and if you do not give me everything that happened that day and what you said you are going to go away."

"Why didn't you tell me this shit before? I mean what am I paying you for if you are not going to inform me?"

"You are paying me to get you out of here. You are paying me that I won't let you go away for a long time. I know what I am doing Chelsea. You need to trust me. Now you need to tell me what I need to hear so we can start!" Rebecca said standing up getting furious turning red in the face.

"I do not understand what I said has anything to do with this case?"

"Ms. Johnson, can you please tell me?" she asked sitting back down and popping open her briefcase and reaching for documents.

"I refuse to say anything. You know what fuck it. I will do five years. If that is what it is going to take I will do five years. This is some bullshit!" Chelsea said sitting back in the chair smiling at Rebecca.

She took her hand out and placed some documents on the table. "You are acting ignorant right now. Chelsea, now I tried to be fair with you, but my job is to win a case. I haven't lost a case yet. I don't plan to now, so what I need you for you to do is read these documents for me. You are not going to be negative right now. We can beat this. If you will work with me I promise you will not do five years. Please just work with me. Jail is nothing like prison. Once those doors are open you are fresh meat."

Rebecca said moving her hair to the left side. "Other inmates will come after you whether it is sexual content or just don't like you and want to fight you. You need to focus and work with me, Chelsea. This is not game. This is real life.

You tried to kill someone and you should have been gone. Now work with me," Rebecca said looking focused into Chelsea's eyes.

Chelsea shook her head yes.

"Great…..now we have the texts messages you sent him on the day of the accident, but before you do please read this letter that was found under your bed a month ago," she said pulling out a yellow notepad and black pen from her briefcase.

Chelsea was shocked. She thought she threw the paper away. She knew reality had set in and knew her lawyer was serious about her being locked up for five years. Tears started to form and her mouth started to twitch in fear. She knew the documents were harsh and could make her go to being a prisoner. She did exactly what Rebecca said and read.

"Okay, I am going to read this and after I read this please tell me what is going to happen. Whatever type of money you need I have a savings…"

"Just read Ms. Johnson."

"The title of this letter that was sent to Brandon Daniels is called, "Your Last Breath Will Be Mine.""

She looked up and down at Rebecca and her breathing was harder. She cleared her throat and started to read the document letter.

"Tormented, this is how my heart and soul feels inside being in this room. We were the perfect couple even though we had to go out of the city and be together when I came there. I really enjoyed our time. We laughed, held hands, and had a child together, but you made me get an abortion, because you wanted us to do it right and be married. It is funny because at the time you and your wife did not have kids and I was about to give you one.

It hurts my heart on how you didn't want our child here. Why Brandon? You could have left her right then when I was pregnant. I was so damn dumb.

I can't believe I almost killed someone for you and now my karma is here in this fucked up ass hell hole while your black ass is probably with her. It is okay because you are going to reap what you sow. I called you the other day. For the first time in a year you finally picked up. Shortly afterward, I realized it was your phone on automatic answer because I heard her and what sounded like a child.

Seems like you two have a baby together now, but guess what I am getting out soon. Now you are scared of Chelsea, you are hurt by Chelsea because she knows now. You and that bitch thought I was going away huh? Well guess what Brandon; you are going to be hurt even more by Chelsea. I am coming after you, Brandon. You are not going to get away for everything you have done.

You think you can just go back to your wife and not make me a wife. Oh hell no.....Oh no, that day is going to come when you think you have gotten away with everything. I am laughing as I write because you don't even know that I am getting out in a month. This letter, I hope it makes it to you before I get there, because if it doesn't good luck in heaven. I am coming after you, Brandon. Fuck the signed by whom. You will be hurt by me and I will be the side chick who turned into your wife.......Chelsea broke down and started to cry.

"Chelsea, that letter....it, was a statement that you were going to go after Brandon and kill him. This is the reason why she testified against you. I had an agreement to get you a lot of probation before this, but when that letter was found it made it even harder for you.

Why Chelsea, why go after him? Why jeopardize what you have gone through for a man?"

"What are you my lawyer or my counselor?" Chelsea asked looking at her with teary eyes.

It was complete silence.

"I am a woman who has been in your situation before. I know what it feels like."

"Did you go to jail? Did you have to be in here with fucked up twisted ass people?"

"No."

"Well you don't know what it's like. I gave this man me for a whole damn year. I waited for him to leave his wife. He promised me that I was going to be his wife. You don't understand I loved this man. Now look at me. I lost a great job and everything. He is smiling and having sex with another woman who is probably going to take my place. I was supposed to be his wife. I was up next to be married not the next bitch. I don't know if he and his wife have a child together. The bitch couldn't have a baby and probably got pregnant all of sudden. Or it might be another bitch.

All I know is someone has his child. He chose me to be his wife! If I would have been calm everything would have happened."

"Chelsea, love isn't like that honey. It isn't. I thought it was just like that. This man wasn't going to leave his wife for you."

"Save your speech lady please. All I need you to do is tell me what is going to happen to me."

Please let me keep talking, as I was saying, he is not going to ever love you. He is lying to you. He will continue to string you alone, because he knows you are a weak woman. You are not a real woman. You are not the type he wants to marry and if he does marry you he will cheat on you. Maybe if he does be with you it's because you were the last thing that wanted him. You need to know your worth."

Chelsea turned her body to the side. "You don't know how it feels to give a man everything and I mean everything."

"Oh I don't? Honey, I do. I was a junior in college at 21, and I thought this man was going to make me his woman. He told me he was going to leave his wife too.

He took me everywhere but to his heart. I had a plan all together that I was going to murder her, because I loved him. He drove me crazy. I wanted to be his wife too, but there was a woman who was. He used me for ass, because the whole time she was moving things into the new house they built in New York. He told me they were separated and she was moving to New York. After I did my homework he moved on me. From that day on I followed my dreams and made sure that I wouldn't lose ever again especially to a man.

You don't understand that I lost so much. I was a junior in college with a 3.8 at Georgia State putting a man in front of my schooling. I could have been just like you but I didn't go that route. I need you to read the next couple of documents for me please. You will read what you sent to Brandon on the plane. Here is 4:45 am central time. Here is another one at 10 43 am Eastern Time. I will do my best to get you out of here."

"Do you promise?"

"I promise. You are now going to read the text you sent to Brandon before you tried to kill his wife."

"Can you stop calling her that please?"

Rebecca sighed, "Okay, Chelsea, I will call her Mrs. Daniels."

"Thank you. Now I will read this."

She cleared her throat and began reading.

"The day you cheated on me is going to be your last. But I cannot go on about it because people are looking and listening. Remember I am number 2 for a reason. Your wife might be in the bed right now but I know where you want to be. You want us together but Brandon seeing you every other day hurts. You can leave her. You two do not have kids together. You already told me that she isn't going to take anything from you. So why Brandon? Why keep stringing me along making me think we will be together. I sit here laughing ready to work the shift. But guess what Brandon?"

She went to the next page.

"Guess what damn it….your wife is aboard this flight. I told her everything. I am going to kill this bitch. I had enough of you giving me shit and this bitch! I have been faithful and just waiting Brandon. I can't wait anymore. You are going to be mine. We just need this bitch out of the way because I don't think she is going to sign those papers. By the time you get this text you better give me an answer at 10:55 pm or I am going to leave her bloody."

"Read the next piece of paper," Rebecca said jotting down notes.

"Damn it Brandon five minutes is up. You think I won't? I am going to kill her now or should I leave her bloody? Pick it…you know what? Fuck this talking. I am going right now…good-bye Brandon until I get to our home. Bye."

Chelsea pushed the documents closer to Rebecca, put one arm on the table and her hand down.

"Chelsea, listen, what you just did was brave. Listen, honey,"

Nurse Tasha walked back in. "Chelsea, it is time."

Chelsea picked her head up and looked at Rebecca distraught.

"Please just give me one more minute with her. Okay?" Rebecca said putting her finger towards Nurse Tasha.

"Okay."

"What made you want to kill her?"

"I heard a voice say, If you kill her he will be yours."

"Okay that is enough," Nurse Tasha said walking over to get Chelsea.

Nurse Tasha grabbed Chelsea's hand.

"I need you to get me out of here before I kill myself," Chelsea whispered and stood up. Rebecca looked sideways at Chelsea as Nurse Tasha grabbed her hand and headed toward the door.

"We are trying to help people in here not rehash what they did," Nurse Tasha said looking mean at Rebecca.

Chelsea and Nurse Tasha walked out of the room and Nurse Tasha closed the door hard. Rebecca never lost a case but she was somewhat skeptical about this one with Chelsea.

Chapter Two

Unbalanced

"Brandon! Brandon! It is time to get up. Come on baby wake up," Vanessa said in a high-pitched voice smacking his big bicep frequently. Vanessa was 5'1 lying on her side naked climbing her tall 6'2 husband. Her tits pressed against his bicep as she watched him wake up. She was thick with a little belly that Brandon loved. Her light skin body had Brandon's hand prints on her ass from being smacked so hard.

Brandon tossed and turned across the lavender Satin king sheets. The black leather soft couch by the TV stand had Brandon's clothes pressed ready for him to put them on.

Vanessa looked at the black clock. "Baby, it is almost 6 am. Okay your flight leaves at 11 am. Baby, come on now. You know that Atlanta traffic is crazy right now and the airport is always busy on a Friday. You don't want to miss your flight.

Brandon opened his eyes grunting and stretching his arms wide. "What time is it?" he asked with a deep strong voice.

"It's 5:45 am. How did you sleep? She said her hazel eyes glued to him waking up.

Brandon sat up with the cover covering his waist below. He smiles and says "too good".

He yawned and stretched. "You definitely put it on me last night. I am only gone for the weekend. You act like I am going to meet someone in two days baby." He smiled with his straight pretty smile.

"I know baby but I hate when you leave me. I need you here with me. You know I just got off my period and I am horny as hell. You just got that fresh cut showing your black deep waves and your beard; Oh my God! Baby, I am so happy to be married to a sexy man like you!" she said giving him a hug.

"So you need it huh?" Brandon asked kissing on her dolphin tattoo on her shoulder.

"Yeah, momma needs it. I want more but you have to go. I see that morning wood looking at me. She said wanting to milk him.

He smiles and kissed her again. "Are you sure?"

She laughed. "If you can nut in ten minutes you can have all the pussy you want. I don't want you to be late."

Fuck that meeting. I am here with my gorgeous wife. Five minutes is all I need."

"Whatever....come get this wet pussy."

"Yes." She pulled the sheets off him watching his dick laying on his right upper thigh. Both of his hands laid flat on the bed sitting up. She began to lay flat on his leg showing her nice shapely plump brown skin ass. She sucked his dick. Saliva wet his dick and her mouth massaged him getting him hard with every wet stroke. His head fell back gently with the feeling of excitement.

He looked up towards the white ceiling fan and shook his head. His toes curled constantly. Once she noticed that she circle stroked his dick. He exhaled lightly and her eyes were closing with enjoyment from his dick and noises. She took his dick out of her mouth and jacked his dick and watched his balls follow. .

"Does that feel good baby?" she asked trying to look up at him with her brown Chinese looking eyes.

"Fuck yes it does!" he said laying back. Her smile stole his soul and returned it back. She watched his chocolate body contract every time she gave him a stroke and sucked it. She watched his eight packed abs go in and out. His hairless body she loved. Brandon's dick grew ten inches rocked hard. Brandon looked down to see why she had stopped. She grabbed his dick and got up and straddled his long shaved dick. Slowly he entered into her wet, warm, tight pussy. She moaned soon as he entered and couldn't go anymore. She leaned forward on his chest with her hands on the bed. Brandon grabbed and smacked her ass. He guided her slowly up to the tip and back down to the base. She started to ride him faster with her luscious ass clapping as she rode him.

"Damn Brandon, that fucking big ass dick in my pussy. God you have some good ass dick. Go ahead and grip my ass and fuck me nigga!" she said looking into his eyes ready to be slam fucked.

Brandon took control and wrap both hands around her back and started to fuck her. His balls grew smaller ready to let cum out of them soon.

"God….this pussy is so fucking good! Shit!" he said biting his teeth. "You are going to make me cum in this pussy. Shit!" He leaned his face towards to the right side feeling so good.

"You want to nut in this pussy?" she asked holding her short Fantasia hair cut so it wouldn't be all wild.

"I am going to cum," his breath stammered.

"Go ahead and cum, baby. This is your pussy." She moaned loudly feeling his balls hit her pussy.

"Shit!" Brandon let loose inside of her. He pumped two more times to make sure he got all of his cum out.

"Is that all of it?" she asked rolling over to the right side of the bed.

"Whew…yes…shit!" he said trying to catch his breath.

"Good. Baby, I am really sorry," Vanessa said sitting up starting to get emotional.

"Baby, what is wrong?" he asked alertly rushing to her side.

"I know when you cum in me…you want a baby and I can't give you a baby," she added for him to hold her.

He held her. "Oh no, baby. Don't do this before I go."

"We have tried everything and nothing is working. I am so sorry baby. I feel like a failure" she cried.

"Come on baby, I promise when you go to the doctor today they are going to give you some great news. I know I can't be there but baby I will be there with you in spirit. I know everything is going to go fine. Watch!"

"I really wish you can go with me. I need you in my life. I want you by my side."

"I know you do baby, but you know I have that meeting and I have to make this one. If I get this deal my salary is going to go up and you know what that means right?" he asked with excitement.

"We can get patio furniture."

"Yes! I promise baby, this is our year. This is our season. God is going to bless us in ways watch. You just have to have faith that is all."

"I am trying to have it baby, but…."

"But nothing baby, we didn't get this far by ourselves. God was with us. He gave us this house. He is the one that put us together. We have been together with each other for eleven years and married eight years.

And you know sometimes I can't stand you" he laughed being hit by her with a smile.

"At the end of the day I love you. I keep telling you that it isn't what man says. It is about what God says. Man will just confirm the victory for us. Can I get amen?" he asked leaning his ear over for a response.

"You are silly," she laughed placing the sheets over her. "Go ahead and get ready."

"Yeah. It is going to be a long day. I can feel it," he said getting out of bed with a long eight inches while soft going straight down.

"Hmmmm....it is very long. You know I want to drain that dick again but my pussy is starting to hurt now" she laid down caressing her pussy lips.

"Pussy shouldn't be good." He grabbed his phone off of the night stand and walked off to the bathroom to run the shower.

Vanessa's phone went off of the wooden nightstand next to her. She grabbed it by the picture of her and Brandon in their wedding dress and suit. Darren was across the screen.

She double looked and answered it.

"Hey," she talked lowly.

Brandon walked back in the room.

"Hey Darren, what's up?" Vanessa said loudly.

Brandon looked at her viciously and grabbed his baby blue briefs.

"Yeah, I come to work tonight at eight, that's right. Okay, I will see you there. Okay, bye bye now." She pressed end.

"What the hell was that about?" he asked looking at her with his hand to the side and his long chocolate dick swinging to each thigh when he walked closer to the bed.

"It was Darren. He was just asking if I am coming in today that's all. I didn't want to pick up because I knew you were going to trip."

"You damn right. You know I do not like that guy. Why do you keep talking to him?"

"Brandon, he was engaged to my cousin last year. You must have forgotten he found out last year that his three year old daughter isn't his. Now she is pregnant and it probably isn't his. He has been through a lot. So he came back home and he is a Deacon at my church. He also works at the hospital with me too. I don't know why you don't like him. He is a pretty good guy," she said standing up heading to the dresser mirror to look at herself.

"Because Vanessa, he is a sneaky guy."

She laughed. "Why is he sneaky, Brandon?"

"He looks sneaky. I mean why did he move back here for?"

"He has family here, that's why. He wanted to come home. I promise he hasn't tried me or anything. He is just a co-worker and a church member."

He just an old coon looking for some ass now! Isn't he like 40 years old?"

"So what is your point?" she asked with her hand on her hip.

"You're 32 about to turn 33 in August baby. He is way too old to be hanging around you."

"Why are you trying to sound like my daddy for?"

"I'm not. I just don't like it and why is he calling you 6:33 in the morning then asking if you are coming in?"

She turned around. "Because the rest of the people at our job are full of drama and have depressing stories, and besides he likes one of the women at my job."

"I still don't like it. I don't trust this guy one bit. I am about to get in the shower" he walked off in the bathroom to take a shower. Vanessa blew a sign off relief. She knew he didn't like Darren, but she loved when he gets mad and jealous. It turned her on. She went into the drawer and grabbed a white bra and striped white and pink cotton panties to put on. She put them on slow because her pussy was sore. She laid on the bed, grabbed the remote and turned the 32 inch TV on.

Brandon took a shower. He was excited about his trip. He got out of the shower and his phone lit up. He checked it and smiled. He started to brush his teeth and opened the door with a white towel around his waist.

He muffled. "No one wants to see you with them grandma panties on" he laughed from the picture she sent to his phone.

She laughed. "You like it though."

He chuckled and walked back into the bathroom to finish getting ready.

After a couple of minutes, Brandon started to get dressed. He put on a black suit, a dark blue dress shirt and black dress shoes on. Vanessa watched as he got dressed.

"One thing I love is watching you in a suit. You are turning me on right now," she said getting aroused.

He brushed his hair. "I look good to be 34 years old don't I?"

"Hell yeah, I want to fuck you again, but my pussy is so sore."

He walked over to her side of the bed and kissed her on the forehead.

"Well when I get back maybe it will be healed. I want you to ride my face and let your cum drip down to my mouth."

"Brandon go now." She smiled getting turned on.

'Alright I am going. I will see you when I get back right?" he said giving her a hug.

"Yes, baby, please call me as soon as you get there."

"I got you baby. I love you."

"I love you too."

Brandon walked out of the bedroom to the stairs and out of the door.

He got into his 2007 black F-150 and drove to get a quick sausage biscuit and hash brown from McDonald's. The temperature on a June 3, 2012 day outside felt great. He rolled his windows down to feel the breeze as she prepared his meeting in Houston. He finally arrive to the airport went to park his car and went into the airport. The airport was packed. He went inside to go through TSA and etc to get to his gate. What Brandon didn't realize going to Houston, this time was going to change his life.

Chapter Three
Meeting Chelsea

After waiting two and half hours it was time for Brandon to board the plane. He stood up and waited to hear his gate number. He looked around at the numerous people at the airport. He heard his gate and walked in line. He walked to the gorgeous Hispanic customer representative woman and handed his e-ticket. She ripped his end and looked up and smiled at Brandon. Brandon walked to the ramp smelling the outside weather of Atlanta.

He walked to the plane and he saw a beautiful brown skin flight attendant standing next to the pilot. They were greeting all the passengers that boarded the plane. Brandon smiled really hard as she locked eyes with him.

He read her name tag Chelsea and turned right to walk to his seat. He couldn't stop thinking about her smile as he walked to the middle of the plane and put his duffle bag in the overhead bin. His seat was on outside of the aisle. Brandon stared at the front to watch her. He watched her smile at every passenger coming in. He looked at her plump butt poking out of her navy long skirt.

He looked at her slim figure as her flight attendant outfit fit perfectly on her. He loved his wife but he had a thing for slim brown skin women with long hair. Her hair wrapped into a ponytail. A young black man walked and wanted to get in his seat.

Brandon stood into the aisle and let him in. He sat back down and look to his right where he saw an elderly woman looking at him.

"Honey, you have been looking at her since you've got on the plane," the woman said titling her head showing her eyes through her glasses.

"Yes ma'am, she is very nice looking. For some reason I cannot take my eyes off of her," he said smiling at her yet still looking at the flight attendant.

"Well, you need to because from the looks of it you are married. Am I right?"

Brandon looked at his ring and his emotions were shot. "Yes ma'am, I am with a gorgeous wife, but you know I am just looking at her."

"If you were a good man you would send your wife a text letting her know she is gorgeous and that you will see her soon or when you get back," the elderly woman said looking away and adjusting her seat.

Brandon didn't care about what she was saying. He couldn't take his eyes off of the flight attendant and wanted to hear her voice. His phone started to vibrate. He thought he turned it on airplane mode. The intercom came on telling everyone to put their electronic devices on airplane mode and to turn off their laptops. He grabbed it and checked to see who it was.

The elderly woman said "mmm". Brandon looked at her with a sideways glance. He looked at his phone and it was his wife sending him a picture of her ass that covered his whole screen. Brandon gazed at it as the flight attendant he couldn't take his eyes off said "sir, can you please turn your phone on airplane mode."

Brandon was startled and dropped his phone.

"Sir, I am so sorry to scare you," she said bending down getting his phone. She grabbed it and looked up and smiled. Brandon looked at her and blinked fast to save the image of her gorgeous face in his mind.

"Here you go," she said standing up and walking towards the back of the plane.

"Thank you," he said turning around to look at her switch. He looked back at the picture and closed it to turn the airplane mode on. After a couple of minutes the flight attendants got in the middle of the aisle to show the passengers how to use the equipments and instructions on the plane.

The flight attendant was right next to Brandon and he looked at her. He smelled her nice fragrance. He knew he was married but this woman was something special.

He thought about fucking her brains out. She looked to the side of him and smiled again. Brandon knew that she liked him after all the smiles she was giving him. He put his seatbelt on and the plane started to move. The flight attendants started to get in their positions to prepare for takeoff. The young man next to him hit him on the shoulder.

"Bruh, that flight attendant she is bad bruh. She is looking at you too. What you better do is take off the ring bruh and get at her."

He looked down at his ring and thought about taking it off. She had to see it. He didn't want to take it off and show her that he was disloyal to his wife. A couple of minutes the flight attendants came around. Brandon knew he wanted her but didn't know what to expect.

"Sir, would you like anything?" Chelsea said bending down smiling as her fragrance hit his face.

The first thing that came to his mind was fucking her in the bathroom. He knew he couldn't say that.

"Not at this moment, but if you don't mind...what is your name?"

"Chelsea," her voice said angelically. She smiled at him and walked to other passenger.

"She is bad bruh, but you did look like a dumb guy right there. Her name is on her name tag," the young man said putting his hand to his mouth laughing. "Bruh you better say something for real before I bag her."

"How old are you?" Brandon asked fixing his tie.

"I am 22 years old," he said sitting up right. "What is your name bruh?"

"Brandon," he said attending his hand for a shake.

"Anthony," he said shaking Brandon's hand.

"She looks good, but I am just taking my time. She has been smiling at me ever since I got on. It is something about her man."

"I tell you what it is. It is that long hair, slim figure with a fat ass, and do you see her light brown eyes.

Man she is gorgeous. She is the type of woman you want to settle down with and get her pregnant. I bet someone is having fun beating that pussy up when she comes home."

"And I wish I was that guy," Brandon said sitting back in his chair thinking about her. She looked at him and smiled even harder, because she knew he was talking about her.

Brandon and Anthony started to discuss different things on the plane. While they were talking Chelsea walked to the back and bumped her booty into Brandon. He knew right then she liked him.

"I am sorry sir, turbulence," she said smiling even harder. She walked off.

"It is a wrap. Once you get off the plane man you should get at her. I am pretty sure she has to get to another flight or she might live in Houston. I would get at her if I was you. You know damn well it wasn't turbulence," he said turning his head to see if she heard him.

"I think I am definitely going to talk to her after the flight". He said smiling and looking to the side of him.

The elderly woman looked at him with disappointment. After two hours the pilot informed everyone they were about to descend and land in Houston. In Brandon's mind he wanted to know if Chelsea was feeling him.

He knew he had a wife at home and was away on business but a causal conservation is what he wanted from her. The plane hit the ground and pulled into the IAH in Houston. Everyone was cleared to get up and get their luggage and leave the plane. Brandon grabbed his duffle bag and looked back at Chelsea. He whispered to her and nodded his head towards the exit. She smiled and nodded her head yes.

She stayed professional and he smiled. He walked off the plane into the terminal. He waited in the gate lobby for her. He turned his airplane mode off. He had several messages. He had one from one of his coaches at Georgia Central Flyers that he was supposed to have lunch with a client at 5:30 pm. He looked at the time and it was 12:55 pm. He went through his messages and answered back. After his last message he was about to text "I miss you" he felt a tap on his shoulder. He turned around and it was Chelsea.

"I am so sorry to keep you waiting," she said with a beautiful low country accent.

Brandon smiled in shock. "No... no... it is okay. I was just answering a few messages. How are you?"

"I am doing well. I am glad to be off. I cannot wait to go home."

Inside of Brandon's mind he felt victory. He knew she had to live in Houston and could not wait for her to confirm.

"You must live here in Houston?"

"Yes, I do. Do you?"

"No, I don't. I live in Atlanta, but I recruit high school and two year college football players. I am a defensive coach at Georgia Central Flyers," he said showing his teeth of happiness.

"You know that is very weird to say," she said switching the hand holding her little suitcase handle.

"Why you say that?"

"I actually went to Georgia Tech and graduated there. I am actually the class of 2008. Wow that is really weird. You must remember me from there or something?"

"Not at all. I am the class of 2004. You were a freshman coming in and I was a senior, so you know I didn't want a little girl at the time. Plus I played football," he said wishing he could take back that comment.

"Hmmm…I can just imagine you in those pants right now. Also that is funny because it seems you want me now? Am I right?"

He chuckled, "I don't know what you are talking about and by the way my name is Brandon Daniels. It is Chelsea again right?"

She pointed to her name tag and laughed. "That's right. Chelsea. It is great to meet you."

"I am so sorry. I am kind of nervous."

"That is okay. I don't know why you are a handsome man."

"Thank you," he paused.

"It is nice to meet you too Brandon. I don't mean to be rude but can we head to the parking lot? I am ready to get out of these heels."

"It is cool I can walk you to the car. Do you want me to carry your suitcase for you?"

"That would be great", she said handing him the suitcase handle. "You don't have any other bags that you have to get do you?"

"No, I don't. I am only going to be here for the weekend? I usually pack light when I come here," he said adjusting his duffle bag on his shoulder.

She looked at his pelvis area sexually and shook her head. "I can see that. Well let's walk this way."

Brandon saw that she was looking and knew she was undressing him with her eyes. They started to walk and Brandon let her walk ahead of him just a few inches.

He watched her hips go side to side as she walked. He knew he was there for the weekend but wanted her right then. He didn't think about his wife until his phone started to ring.

"You better answer that", she said turning her head back.

"It is probably one of the coaches. I will get it soon."

"Or it could be your wife telling you she miss you with another ass picture," she said smiling, turning his head to the front.

Brandon walked with giant fast steps to get side by side. "So you saw that?"

"I am pretty sure a lot of people saw it. You didn't hide it well. I also spotted your ring on your hand." She smiled.

"I am sorry about that."

"What are you sorry about? Are you sorry that your wife sent you an ass picture or that you are married?"

"I don't know. I am confused," Brandon said. He didn't know what to say.

"It is cool, Brandon. You see something that you are attracted too and cannot keep your eyes off of her. It is totally fine."

"So I guess you do not want to have this conservation with me now do you?"

"Well, it is up to you. She is in Georgia right now and you are walking me to my car.

Do you think I have a problem with it? I think I would not be with you if I wasn't okay with it."

Brandon was shocked that she didn't care about him having a wife being so gorgeous.

"Let me ask you something, Brandon. I mean let's be real," she spoke up making sure she heard him as the crowd noise grew.

"Go ahead."

"What is it? Are you tired of her pussy? Is she getting fat? You don't love her? She cheated on you? She doesn't suck dick? What is it?"

"Wow, you are really blunt aren't you?"

"Listen, I get guys like you all the time trying to talk to us flight attendant women. I want to know what it is that she is doing wrong."

Brandon second guessed on saying his real problem. "Well we are about to get a divorce."

"Why is that?"

"She cheated on me with my cousin two years ago. She ended up pregnant but lost the baby when she was three months pregnant. It was just so much to bear with but I stayed with her. She is my wife for eight almost nine years in September. I begged her to have my child but her career kept getting in the way."

"What does she do?" Chelsea asked getting deep into his story.

"She is an RN at Emory hospital in Atlanta."

"That is a great field. Okay, go ahead."

"She kept saying she didn't have time. She loved her job and didn't want to take any time off. She has been on birth control since we have been together. She didn't want her youth to go away, so she tries to send me these pictures to make me forget about what she done to me. I didn't deserve it. I am tired of thinking about how many times she cheated on me or may have. It hurt my heart Chelsea.

I am just tired of going on the road and thinking if she is cheating on me. It is sickening. I had to file for divorce. She won't sign the papers. She wants us to work things out. We signed a prenup so I can keep what I came in the marriage with. I will still give her something but I didn't trust her when I married her," Brandon said pausing a moment in the parking garage.

"Do you two still stay together?"

"For the moment yes, but we sleep in different rooms.

Chelsea felt sorry for Brandon. "If you knew she would cheat on you why did you marry her?"

"Because we started to go to church. God change people. I knew she was going to better herself when she got saved, but those sinful ways came back. Don't get me wrong I love her, but I can't keep going on another year stressed out." He started to get emotional.

"Brandon, I am so sorry to hear that. Wow that is very deep," she said feeling sorry for him rubbing his back.

"Thanks Chelsea, I am sorry if I came on too strong but our love just isn't there and I am trying to be a good man but damn it! I cannot keep doing this to myself. I deserve a good woman in my life. I work hard and I am a great man of God. I deserve a good woman."

"I understand, my ex-boyfriend cheated on me, so I can totally relate," she said getting her keys out of her suitcase and unlocking the door to her white 2012 Honda Accord LX Sedan. "Brandon, do you have a rental car or something?"

'No, I usually take the taxi to my hotel. I am staying at the Hilton across from Toyota Center."

"Okay, great. I stay like ten minutes from there. I can take you there. I would like to talk with you more. I mean it is up to you. I am not going to kidnap you or anything. I hate when a bitter bitch cheats on a good man," she said opening the trunk of her car.

"Thank you so much." He placed her suitcase and his duffle bag in the trunk.

Brandon closed the trunk and they got in the car heading downtown to his hotel. They continued to talk about relationships, careers, the future and exchanged numbers. They arrived in front of the hotel and Chelsea put the car in park looking at Brandon seductively.

"So after your meeting what are you doing later on", Chelsea said taking her ponytail out and letting her hair fall to the middle of her back.

Brandon was surprised by how blunt she was. He was attracted to her. He wanted Chelsea really bad but didn't know if she wanted him, so he gave it a try.

"I am just going to be in my room chillin' unless I get up with one of the coaches tonight. I doubt it because I just want to relax. Like I said the meeting is at 5:30 pm at the restaurant across from the lobby," he said looking up at the big tall building.

"Great. Well I will love to come over at 9 if you don't mind and chill with you. I think you deserve a little fun before you go back to that hell hole. What you think? We can have a couple of drinks at the same place where you will have your meeting."

Brandon leg shifted from getting aroused. "That would be great. What do you have in mind in terms of fun?" he knew he just wanted confirmation.

She licked her lips at him. "Brandon, just be ready at 9 and you will know exactly what I am talking about baby."

They both smiled at each other and then Brandon reached in for a kiss. She kissed him back. The moment was intense grabbing each other necks. They let go from each other.

"I am going to go ahead and check in," he said wiping his lips.

"You do that. I will see you at nine. You don't need any condoms. I want you to fuck this pussy. I want to feel all of you. I got your number so I will be texting you when I am on my way."

Brandon smiled again and opened the door. "See you at nine", he said looking back at her before closing the door.

He closed the door, grabbed his duffle bag and Chelsea drove off. He wished it was 9 already. He turned around to face the building and walked inside. He chuckled with evil because he knew that tonight he was going to have a great evening with Chelsea before going home to his wife in Atlanta.

Chapter Four
My Night with Chelsea

Brandon walked in the hotel to check-in. After he checked in he walked to the elevator to his room. He got to his room, opened the door and started to settle in. He sat on the bed and turned on the TV and then his phone started to ring. It was the client he had to meet from a local college in Houston. He wanted to make sure they were still meeting for dinner. Brandon confirmed not knowing the meeting was in two hours.

All he could think of was Chelsea and having her body on top of his. Her luscious lips plump like Megan Good and her eyes, gorgeous eyes, whispering in his ears made him want her to have his baby.

His phone rang again and it was his wife. He looked at the time and it was 2:15pm. He knew she was pissed. He picked up.

"Hey baby", he said taking his dress shoes off.

"Where are you?" Vanessa asked yelling lying in bed.

"Baby, I am at the room. Why are you yelling?"

"You were supposed to call me when you landed. You know how I feel about you flying on the airplane. Damn it Brandon that is all I ask for. Why can't you just do a simple little thing for me?"

"Vanessa, is it that serious?"

"You must don't see the news with the plane crashing and shit? I mean is it that hard for you to pick up the phone and call your wife to let her know you made it!'

"Brandon exhaled, "you are right. I am sorry baby. I made it."

Vanessa hung up the phone. "Vanessa! Vanessa!" Brandon said pulling the phone from his ear knowing she hung up on him.

"You see that shit right there," he said taking his tie off and throwing it on the bed. He started to take his shirt off and pull his pants down. He had on plaid boxers and rubbed his abs looking into the mirror. His phone rang again and he picked it up from the bed.

"Why didn't you call me back Brandon?" she asked crying into the phone. "I mean all I ask for you to let me know. Is something wrong with that?"

"No, baby, my battery was low. I was on the plane jotting down what I was going to say at the meeting. This guy had 2,000 yards rushing this past season and I am trying to close this deal. I am trying to get him to transfer, I am sorry, but I did get the picture you sent me. I can't wait to get home."

Vanessa wiped her tears and pulled the sheets from her body. She was naked and opened her legs wide.

"Oh yeah, what are you going to do to me?"

"Really you want to do this right now?" he asked pulling his boxers down. He grabbed his dick in his hand and started to jack it. His dick started to grow from six inches from being soft. He started to get hard thinking about Chelsea. He vision he was talking to Chelsea and the things he wanted to do to her. He forgot that he was talking to his wife.

"I want that fat dick to get hard. This pussy is so wet for you right now," she said playing with her clit.

When he heard her voice Brandon rolled his eyes looking at the time. Her voice made him think about her then Chelsea. He wanted to get in the shower and prepare for his meeting especially tonight with Chelsea. "Alright baby, I am going to say a little piece to you. I want you to play with your pussy. I am not going to stop speaking until you cum for me okay," he said taking his hand off his dick. He wanted to save his nut for Chelsea.

"You ready baby."

"Hell yeah", she said moaning with her eyes closed.

"Okay baby, here we go." He lay on the bed with his 10 inches shooting towards the ceiling. He searched for Chelsea's Facebook's page as he talked to his wife.

"I am after you. Now don't let me chase after you. My sex game will get you high. You won't even have to smoke. My touches will make your body shiver. I'm the type to fuck you, suck the cum out of you and after that cook for you. Every day I love to admire your body it's a wonderful sight. Your hair, eyes, thighs, legs, lips, figure, skin, and the way you pose.

Come here baby look into my eyes tell me what you see. I see a man that is about to give you what your body been waiting for. The respect your pussy need and to get all that stress bottle it up and make it cum so I can taste all of it. Hold me; wrap your arms around my neck look into my eyes. Now kiss me your lips taste so soft. I pull you a little closer so you can feel my dick and to get it hard. Our breaths are meeting each other and I can see your body getting weak. You're melting in my arms your hands on my arms feeling my muscles while I kiss under your neck.

As you lay your head back and let out a deep breath. My breaths are deep too. You like how I'm on you and massage your body with my hands. You like my warmth? What you want next? My kisses go down to your chest area licking your smooth skin and I love your smell it just does something to me. I hold your breasts in my hand and lick your nipples and suck on them and blow on them to get hard. Do you like that? Look at me baby, while I kiss on your stomach and kiss your navel; a kiss while you place your hand on my head. On my knees I can smell that fresh pussy begging for attention and ready to be pleased. I'm coming you don't have to beg.

Put your leg on my shoulder and hold on to my head while I taste you with my hands wrapped around your legs. Do me a favor use this hand and spread your pussy lips for me so I can tease her. I give your pussy a kiss and smell it and stick my fingers in your pussy take it out and suck the juices off of my fingers. Oh yeah I am ready to lick so I stick my long tongue out and gently lick your pussy on each lip real slow while you look at me.

How does that feel baby? I see you biting your lips as my hot tongue and breaths on your pussy let my tongue lay across your pussy. My tongue licking your pussy lips while you grip my head tighter and off balance while I let my tongue drag to your thighs. Giving you quick licks and massaging your ass kissing your thighs to your feet. Go ahead and turn around for me baby.

I bend you over with your legs spread, I stand up, start with a smack on your ass, lick the back of your neck. My tongue goes to your neck, to your back, giving you one big lick between your ass crack and pussy. You moan as I spread your ass-cheeks and start to eat you from the back. Holding both of your ass-cheeks while your juices splash on my lips and my nose is wet too. Mmm you taste so good. You want to cum in my mouth? Come on baby, I'm sucking the life out of you because you deserve it; you deserve that cum out of your system. Come on baby splash me with your cum. I can feel your thighs trembling, your body getting weak and see your toes curling. I open my mouth wide and you splash all that cum in my mouth.

You cum a lot for me baby, let me swallow it. Ahhh cheese it's all gone as you fall over yeah baby just like that bend that back just a little. I smack your ass and my dick is hard by the scent of your smell, spread those legs looking at your wet pussy. I stick my dick in…in and out real slow while I watch your pussy trying to pull me back. I look on the side of you and watch your expressions and moans and your body. I let your ass bounce off of my dick and then place my hands on each side of your hips and start to fuck you fast. Your hair flying around I'm looking up towards the ceiling because I knew it was going to be good but not this good you trying to push me away. I bring you back with your back against my chest and lick the back of your neck as you turn to the side and kiss me and look at me.

Oh, your pussy is so wet and hot you got to cum baby okay baby let that cum out for me again. I want all that cum out of your pussy give it to me now baby. Oh shit, yeah, that was good baby, fuck! Damn you just shivering. Lay on your back ma and let me taste you before I get in your pussy. I'm going to stick my tongue out and dump my whole tongue in your pussy and suck all the remaining cum out of you while I look at you and you look up towards the sky with your stomach moving up and down and whimpering."

Vanessa's moans started to get louder and her stomach rising up and down. She played with her clit faster and faster and she became wetter. She thought about everything Brandon was saying.

"You want me to fuck you ma? Okay I'll take my tongue out, get on top of you, go ahead and stick it in. Oh, shit that shit kind of tickle. I guess because you so wet, in and out, slowly kiss me and while our breaths are deep. Kiss the tats on my neck and suck on it go ahead

49

it's yours baby don't be afraid while I cuff your ass and bring you closer so I can dive deep in your pussy. I can reach the bottom, your g-spot screaming, crying, and erupting that entire stress, go ahead mama. Your nails engrave on my back go ahead leave your mark let me know how this dick really is. It's good huh? Say my name while I stroke you even faster. Shit your pussy is so wet oh, shit you got to cum mama I see your legs shaking.

Let me get deeper, deeper, and deeper come on baby cum for me oh that was good huh let me eat that pussy up. I get out of your pussy and lick all the reminder of the cum. Damn your toes curling. You want to ride my dick huh come on you hold my dick while you get on top. Shit oh that feels good. Grinding your hips on that dick getting me deeper in your pussy while you push my hands back and lick on my chest and suck on my nipples while you look at me all freaky.

Oh, your pussy juice just falling down my thighs to my balls and to my legs and you wrap your arms around my neck and suck on my neck.

Your ass just bouncing off my dick just clapping on that dick and I can hear that pussy telling me that she got to cum. I grab control and grab your ass-cheeks and start to fuck you baby yeah nothing but dick in you huh? You like that shit? Kiss me. Spanking your ass shit baby you going to make me cum. Shit you got to cum too. I want you to cum before me. Shit get it baby get yours fuck shit I can't hold it baby I pull out and cum on your ass.

My breaths are deep and yours are too. I'm sweating. Your hair is everywhere and you kiss me. Bad thing about this it was all a damn nightmare because I thought I was really giving you what you need and what I need. To my secret admirer I am here baby just waiting on you. Hope you know it's you I'm after. She came right on her fingers and her body froze.

"How was that baby? Are you good now?" he asked looking at the time ready to get off the phone.

"Yes, I am good. I love when you do pieces for me. Go and enjoy your dinner and close the deal. This pussy will be waiting on you."

"I know it will. I will call you later on tonight baby. I love you."

"Brandon, I love you too."

"Brandon, wait."

"Yeah."

"That poem. It felt like you were thinking about someone else.

Brandon had to come up with something fast. "Baby, remember when I met you on campus. I did an FBI search on you. Even though I was a very popular in football there I went to your Facebook's page and was a little nosey. I never told you that, but you finally got out of me."

"Wow. You never told me. You were a stalker for real because I wonder how every time I turned around you would be in the same building as me."

He smiled. "I wasn't stalking. I was interested in you. Don't even trip like that. I am about to take a nap before the meeting. Time is already moving. I will talk to you later baby."

"Okay baby, I love you."

"Love you too."

He hung up the phone and looked at Chelsea's profile picture on Facebook. He couldn't see any other pictures and didn't want to add her to seem crazy.

"Damn Chelsea, you are so sexy," he said to himself.

"I really hope you are serious about coming back to my room because if you are I am going to fuck the shit out of you." He smiled with an evil laugh.

He closed out of Facebook and started to get things ready for the meeting. After he was done laying his clothes out, ironing, and preparing for questions and answers for the meeting he took a nap. He put his phone on silence. He set the room alarm clock for 4:30pm. He went to sleep. An hour and 45 minutes later he woke up. He woke up before the alarm clock. He disabled it and turned his phone back on to sound.

He had no messages. Which he was surprised at. Minutes later he ran his shower and text Chelsea his phone.

"Hey, what I was thinking was we should have dinner and a couple of drinks in your hotel room. I think it would be better and break the ice doing everything in your room, and after that if you are a cool guy you can come back to my place. I have a pool and I want to see you get wet every which way. Are you cool with that?"

Brandon texted back, "Yes." He smiled really hard ready for her.

"K."

He clapped his hands together in excitement and jumped in the shower. He started to think about him and Chelsea together in the shower.

The water ran across his chocolate body. He placed his head down letting the water hit the top of head. He closed his eyes and thought about being at her place. He thought about her riding his dick. Brandon shook his head to focus.

He wanted Chelsea badly, but knew his main focus was the meeting. He washed his body and got out of the shower. He started to get ready for his meeting. His phone rung and it was his client saying he was there in the lobby waiting. He was thirty minutes early but very happy about having a feature with Georgia Central Flyers. Brandon finished getting ready and headed downstairs to meet him.

He met with his client and they went into the restaurant to the bar. They had a very nice meeting. They ordered food and drinks and the client said he was going to transfer.

Brandon called his coach and told him and gave the client his phone. The client was on his phone and Brandon felt a breeze with a tap. He looked to the right and no one was there, but when he looked to his right he saw Chelsea walking past him waving with a smile.

She was dazzling in a tight black dress that hugged every curve of her slim figure and inches down from her pelvis. Her tits poked up with her ass sitting just right in the dress. She clucked every time she walked in her six inch black heels. All the men at the bar were looking at her. Brandon's mouth was wide open. The client took his mouth from the phone and looked at it as well.

"When you are done with coach just give the bartender my phone. I got to handle that," Brandon said getting up and walking toward Chelsea.

The client nodded his head still looking at Chelsea saying no words.

Brandon walked over there buttoning up his gray suit jacket. He smiled and she lifted her head up and smiled back. He sat next to her and couldn't wait to get her out of that dress.

"My God, Chelsea you look amazing. I thought I was supposed to call and let you know or you were going to call me or something," he said giving her a hug and sitting down.

"Well, I got a little bored at home, so I decided I wanted to have a couple of drinks and wait on you. You are looking good too. I love your waves and beard. I love a man with a beard," she said smiling and moving her hair to the right side of her ear.

"Is that right? Well that is great to hear. You know you have all the guys' attention here even the gay bartender."

Chelsea looked at the men at the bar smiling. Some of the women were rolling their eyes. The bartender walked over handing Brandon his phone.

"Will you be sitting here now sir?"

"Um yeah. You can give me a 151 and Coke and what do you want?" he asked putting his phone in his pocket.

"I will take a Margarita with no salt," she said opening up her pocketbook to get her debit card out.

"Oh no, it is on me. I have a tab open. Put your card away."

"Thank you."

"I will be paying for everything she orders okay?"

"Very well sir, ok, I will be right back with your drinks. If you need anything here are some menus," he said handing them a menu and walking off to prepare their drinks.

"So Miss Chelsea, please tell me some things about you. I mean anything.

Where you are from? Do you have any kids? You know things to that nature."

"Someone is being a little nosey aren't they?"

"I mean since we are new friends we should get to know each other. I want you to be comfortable around me."

"I guess," she said chucking with a little blush. "Well my name is Chelsea, I am 30 years old. I turn 31 next month July 26. I am single. I have no crazy ex-boyfriends, I have no kids. I graduate from Georgia Central in 2008 like I said earlier. I am from Houston Texas. I am the only child."

"No crazy ex-boyfriend huh? How long have you been single?"

"I have been single for six months now."

"And you are telling me he is not stalking your gorgeous self?"

She smiled. "Nope. He isn't. That is crazy isn't it?"

"Sure is, but go ahead."

"The last time I had sex was eight months ago."

"Eight months ago and you had a man?" Brandon said placing his right hand on his right leg.

"Yes, I knew he was cheating on me so I banned sex until I caught him. Soon as I banned sex that is when I got a call from one of his co-workers saying they were fucking. She was very bold because she wanted him so bad. She was fucking him but she wanted him as her boyfriend. I let it go. I broke up with him and the next day I wanted things to work out, but he let me know that she was pregnant. I couldn't go back to that.

It hurt because we were together for four years. I thought we were going to be together and get married. It really hurt me for months and still does now," she said placing her hands on her head looking down on the bar.

"Hey….hey…don't let that dirt bag make you feel bad. You are a very gorgeous woman. I think you are a good woman, and any guy will be lucky to have you."

"You think so?" she said getting some joy back into her spirit.

"Yes, I know so. Hey, let's drink to a season of depression being gone," he said grabbing his drink from the bartender.

"Here you guys go. Is there anything else I can get for you?" the bartender said handing them their drinks.

"That is good. Remember to put everything on my tab."

"Very good sir, I will come back to check on you guys in a little bit," the bartender walked off.

"Do you like living in Houston?" he asked sipping his drink.

"I do. I have been here all of my life. It is a great place to be."

"Yeah, I love it too. Your family stays this way right?"

"Yes, my mom. She actually lives three minutes from me. My dad I don't know who he is. He left my mom when she was pregnant with me. Until this day I still don't know who my dad is."

"Oh wow, I am so sorry to hear that."

"It is okay. I have learned to live with it."

"When you went to Georgia Central what was your major?"

"It was Mass Communications."

"Oh wow, so was mine. It is kind of weird we have so much in common."

"It is," Chelsea said feeling her drink and getting a little wet.

She uncrossed her legs so Brandon could see her black panties.

"But enough about me please tell me more about you, Brandon," Chelsea said sipping her drink without a straw.

"Well, I pretty much told you my life now. I am the defensive coordinator at Georgia Tech for about three years now."

"I haven't been to that school since I graduated let alone the city. We used to party so hard. I am sorry but go on."

"It is okay. I am 34 years old and my birthday is actually Tuesday coming up."

"Is that right?"

"Yes, it is."

"What is something you want for your birthday?" she asked moving closer to Brandon.

"Well, I know I want you."

"Good answer, because you are going to get me the whole weekend if you want me."

"Yes, I would love that."

"Good," she said finishing her drink. "Brandon, I am ready to go to my place. I am ready to suck and be fucked good!"

"Check please," he said without hesitating for the bartender to come over.

"So are we going to upstairs or your place?"

"I want to take you back home to my place."

They talked more until he got the check and signed it. They stood up and headed to her car. Chelsea held his hand. The sun was setting and she felt comfortable with him. They got in her car and drove to her place. Brandon's phone was on silent and Vanessa called his phone three times. He grabbed his phone and saw the missed phone calls from her.

"Is that her calling you?" Chelsea asked squinting her eyes.

"Yeah it is. I will call her back," he said putting the phone back into his pocket.

"You won't tonight, because you will be completely drained tonight."

Brandon smiled and loved what she was saying but knew his wife was going to be pissed from him not answering her calls. They were feeling good after a couple of drinks. They pulled up to a two story brick house. They both got out of her car.

They walked into her house. It was nice and the same fragrance she wore lingered in her house. They went into the living room. Brandon went to sit on the couch while she went into the room for something when she yelled "do you know how to swim?"

"Yeah I do…why?"

"Good!" She came out in her see-through black thong and bra.

"Let's go out to the pool," she said standing looking at Brandon.

"Damn. Okay," he said. He didn't know if he should get undressed then.

She walked to the sliding door. "Brandon you know what I want you to do?"

"What?"

She chuckled. "Get out of those clothes. My pool hates clothes. I will be waiting outside" she walked outside.

Brandon took his clothes off real quick and said "you ain't got to tell me twice."

He walked outside in his boxers and saw her thong on the ground. The lights were lit by the five foot pool. The moon was out and the night was beautiful.

"Didn't I say no clothes Brandon? You are very hard headed. This is why you are going to get some good pussy to get some act right in you". She said looking at the big bulge in his boxers.

He pulled his boxers down. Brandon didn't know if she was going to like his big dick or be scared of it.

She looked at his fat long ten inches moving up and down when he pulled his boxers off and threw them on the ground.

"Damn nigga you got a big ass dick."

Brandon smiled. Do you like?"

"Hell yeah. I never had a dick that fuckin' big. Bring your horse dick ass over here. Don't be scared."

He walked over and got in the pool. The water was kind of warm. She came his way with her hair wet lying on her back flat.

"You know what my wish is and I hope you can make it come true."

"What was it?

"It was me and you having sex and recording it. I love to work out and I haven't done it today. Let's just say it's going to be our sex workout tape."

"Chelsea, are you serious? You know I can't do nothing like that. I am a coach and I have a wife. Are you trying to get me in trouble?"

"Who is going to know? I am a flight attendant, baby."

"I can't do that."

"Okay, how about this. How about we record it and erase it after we watch it? I never have done anything like this before. I think it will be sexy watching us on tape." Brandon couldn't resist her sexiness.

"Do you promise you will erase it after we are done?"

She got closer to him wrapping her arms around his neck and giving him peck kisses.

"I promise baby. I will erase it and you can see it when I do."

"Okay let's do it," Brandon said getting harder.

"I feel your dick getting harder. It is time to give you some pussy," she said getting out of the pool and walking to the camera, which was on the chair by the pool.

"Oh shit baby it is so dark over here. It needs light!"

Brandon looked at her strangely because even if he probably didn't agree to record she probably would have anyway.

"The lights from the pool and the light on the camera it will be fine. I am going to bring it over there and one of us can switch holding it or however we do it." She walked over with the camera. "Now go ahead and get on the edge of the steps so I can suck your long meat," she said sitting on the edge of the pool.

With no hesitation Brandon got on the edge of the steps. She handed him the camera so he can record her sucking his dick. He knew Chelsea was a freak especially being tipsy.

She started to suck his dick. She took his long dick to the back of her throat. Brandon was impressed with how much dick she could take in her little mouth. She stood up and shook her ass.

"You like the way I suck your fat dick and balls?"

"Hell yeah, shit!" Brandon said wanting her to keep sucking it. "I am having a hard time holding the camera.

"I am working out my head and hands now I want this dick inside of me. I want to work my ass and thighs. Go ahead and sit down."

Brandon sat down still holding the camera. She spread his legs and turned around and sat on his long dick. He wanted to drop the camera but she said "hold that camera baby don't drop it." She started to ride his dick up and down nice and slow. Brandon was getting every moment feeling her tight wet pussy. It was better than his wife. Up and down she went holding onto his knees. His toes started to curl up because of the hot and tight pussy she was giving him. She looked back at the camera and said "Brandon your dick feels good. This is the biggest dick I'd ever had."

She rode him for about twenty minutes. She was really working Brandon out.

"I want you to put that camera down back on the chair and fuck me from the back."

"Do you want me to still record it?"

"No you can turn it off, just hurry up and give me that long dick."

She stood up wiping the water off of her body and shaking her ass. Brandon got up to put the camera back on the chair. He turned it off and got back in the pool. She stood up leaning over the rail by the steps. Brandon came down the steps and got behind her. He jacked his long dick to get back harder.

"Do you need me to suck it so you can get rock hard?" she asked looking back at him.

"No, I want it to grow in you."

"Okay daddy".

Brandon wrapped his hands around her hips and slid in her sweet wet pussy.

"'Oh your dick and the water feel so good…fuck me Brandon."

Brandon started to give her fast hard back shots. The water was moving every stroke he gave her. Brandon looked at the camera to make sure he turned it off.

"It is off daddy. The red light would have been on," she said sitting up looking back at him. "Oh my God. I am in love with your dick and your abs look so good," she said placing her hand on his abs.

Brandon loved every stroke he gave her but felt his cum coming. He stopped. "I want you out of the pool and on your back."

She grabbed his dick and took him out of her real slowly so he could feel the wetness. She got out and went to the chair to grab a towel and put it on the ground. After she laid the rainbow towel on the ground she got on her back with her legs up.

Brandon couldn't believe how freaky she was. He got on top of her and started to fuck the shit out of her. She grabbed his ass.

"Throw that dick baby! Fuck!" she moaned and yelled.

Brandon knew he wasn't going to last any longer.

"Baby I can see your expressions. You got to cum for me?" she said grabbing her tits and licking them. "Oh Brandon I want you to cum on my face."

Brandon couldn't take any more of her voice and pussy he had to nut.

"Bring me your face then."

She sat up and Brandon quickly pulled out. He stood up and came all over her face and tongue. He was breathing hard.

"Oh my God. Damn that felt good."

She was laughing watching him shake. She grabbed his dick and started to suck more cum out of him. She lifted his balls up and started to suck on them to push more cum to his dick.

"Now that was my protein shake." They both laughed.

"You have some good ass pussy he said bending down feeling exhausted.

"Thank you. That was a workout for real but I am going to be ready to go again in a little bit."

Brandon liked all her sex attributes.

"Do you want anything to eat or drink?" she asked with cum on her face.

"I will take a water."

"Come on in and get you one. I have to wash this cum off of my face. You taste good though." Chelsea asked to be helped up.

Brandon grabbed her hand and she stood up. She started to walk towards the sliding door to go inside.

Brandon paused to look at her fat ass. After she got him a water, he went in her room to take a nap. Chelsea started to cook food in the kitchen. He knew what he did was a sin, but didn't know once you go against the Lord's commandments something was going to happen to him....And what happened is Brandon met Chelsea....

Chapter Five

Go Ahead and Say It

Brandon was drained. It was 10:32pm and Vanessa called his phone four times since he has been at Chelsea's house. Brandon woke up from his nap naked smelling bacon being cooked. He wiped his eyes with the silk covers on him. Brandon leaned over to get his phone out of his pants pocket. He saw the missed calls from his wife and other people. Chelsea walked in with a light blue silk robe. She grabbed her hair and put it in a ponytail. She walked over to him smiling at him and giving him a kiss.

"Did she call again?" she asked stepping back looking at herself in the mirror.

"Yeah she did. I was just about to call her. Do you mind?" Brandon said ready to call Vanessa, but scared.

"Sure. I came in here to let you know I was cooking breakfast. How do you want your eggs?"

Brandon looked at her body in the mirror. "I would love them scrambled."

"Scrambled it is," she said smiling and walking out of the room closing the door.

Brandon made sure she was gone and pressed send to call his wife. The phone rang one time and Vanessa picked up yelling.

"Where the fuck are you?" she asked yelling over the phone.

"I told you I had a client Vanessa. You know I do not take any calls when I am with a client."

"Bullshit Brandon, you had a meeting at 5:30 there and your meetings do not last that long. You know I had an appointment with the doctor. I wanted you to be here. But you don't give a damn about that. You didn't even call to see how it went. It sounds like you are just waking up. You are a fucking ass, Brandon."

"I had a long meeting with this guy. You need to remember he is a grown man not a high school student, so he can stay out late. And I know about the doctor today baby but I am sorry I had way too many drinks. I came upstairs and crashed. What did Dr. Sherman say?"

"It is like you don't even care about this marriage sometimes."

"Vanessa cut the bull and tell me what the man said."

"Okay. You promise you're not going to hate me?"

"Vanessa, I love you baby through sickness and health. I will always stick by your side. I stuck by your side when both of my parents got in a car accident and died three years ago. You should know I am here baby no matter what, so please tell me what he said."

"Brandon.....I am not going to be able to have kids. He said there was no possible way I would ever. We had a chance two years ago, when I was fertile enough. I don't know what to do baby," Vanessa said crying heavily over the phone.

"Oh baby, no....no....shhhh....everything is going to be alright," he said standing up with his hand on his head looking into the mirror.

"Everything is not going to be alright! You are going to leave me. I can't give you a baby. Do you understand I won't be able to give you a little me or a little you? Why would you want to stay with me? You are going to leave me." She broke down crying.

"Vanessa, I don't know why you think that. Baby, I am not going to leave you baby. Why do you keep saying that?"

"Because you told me a couple years ago that you wanted kids. Now since Dr. Sherman finally confirmed it that I won't be able to I know you are going to leave me. Baby, please don't leave me."

"I am not going to leave you. Please calm down. I love you okay and just because the doctor said so doesn't mean God said no. He has the finally word. Calm down baby we will have a baby. It is going to be at the right time. We just have to continue to keep praying and keep trying. Faith and prayer will make our baby. Watch what happens. "

"Okay, baby, when you get home we are going to pray right?"

"Yes we will. I love you."

"I love you too. Brandon, I am sorry baby."

"Hey, we will let God handle it. It is not our battle."

"Okay baby, what are you doing now?"

"I am just at the hotel chillin. I am kind of tired right now. I am just waking up from a nap, but I think I am going to go back to sleep. But listen to me I need you to be strong right now, okay?

You have to be strong and stay positive because we will have this baby. I promise."

"Okay, baby, thank you for being so positive. I love you. I am so sorry to react with anger all the time."

"I know baby. With everything that is going on I totally understand."

"I am going to open a bottle of wine and look at a movie."

"Okay, babe, I love you too. Good night my queen," Brandon said kissing her funny.

"You are so silly. Good night baby." She hung up laughing.

Brandon hung up and started to respond to the text messages he got. Chelsea walked in and Brandon was in shock at the amount of food she cooked. It looked very good. She walked in with eggs, bacon, grits, sausage, and orange juice.

"Damn...that looks good and so do you," he said lying back in the bed and back against the headboard.

"Thank you so much! You need to get some food in you before we go again," she said handing him the plate and orange juice.

"You want some of this dick?"

"Yes, I do. I am going to suck your dick until you cum in my mouth and then you can fuck me again," she said smiling and lifting her eyebrows aroused.

Brandon was in shock by what she was saying and started to eat his food right away. He placed the orange juice on the black night stand. Chelsea walked into the bathroom taking her robe off. Brandon looked at her and heard his phone vibrate. It was a text message. He didn't flinch because he was too busy looking at Chelsea looking at herself in the mirror. She turned to the side and rubbed her plump booty. Brandon ate his food quickly and took two bites of the sausage and one piece of the bacon.

Chelsea turned the light off and walked back towards the bedroom. She saw that he was almost finished with his food. She got in the bed and pulled the light brown sheets back from him. She lay right on the side of Brandon and grabbed his 10 inch dick and placed it to the back of her throat. Brandon put the plate on the nightstand and laid back getting his dick sucked. She took his dick from her mouth.

"I am going to suck your dick until you cum on my face and mouth.

Your balls are big so you have a lot of cum ready to come out again," she said stroking his dick.

Brandon's head fell back to the headboard feeling the hot wet mouth of Chelsea. Chelsea sucked it until she felt his legs quiver ready to nut.

"I want you to stand up so I can catch your nut," she said getting on her knees on the bed.

Brandon stood up and Chelsea started to stroke his dick and suck it. Brandon looked down at her and she looked up at him. His face became tight when he was ready to cum.

"Are you ready to cum?"

He shook his head and jacked his dick. His toes started to curl and her tongue was out flat waiting to catch his load. He could feel the heat coming towards his dick.

"I want you to cum right on my face and tongue baby. Go ahead and paint my face. You want to nut on my face baby?"

"Yes," he said stroking it slow and shot his load on her face and tongue. His cum started to fall on the bed, her chest, and drip down the side of her face.

"Good boy. Are you all out?"

"Yes," he said holding his dick and breathing hard.

She grabbed his dick and started to suck all his nut out.

"Okay, great. You taste really good. I am going to wipe my face off and let you relax a bit then you can get some of this pussy," she said getting out of bed and Brandon watching her ass switch.

He was stunned because he never had a freak like that. He checked his phone from getting it off of the floor. He saw a picture that made him smile and put the phone back down.

Chelsea and Brandon had sex again and he spent the night over there. The next morning she woke him up with head and more breakfast. Brandon loved the type of woman she was. They decided they were going to spend the day together since he had to leave tomorrow.

They got dressed and she took him back to the hotel. Later that morning, Brandon called his wife and made other calls. After he was done he laid back down until he was woken by a text from Chelsea. She was letting him know that she was going to pick him up at 4pm. He texted back letting her know that was great.

Brandon relaxed for the remainder of the day. He did more work to strengthen his defense for training camp. Later on in the afternoon Brandon got dressed and she picked him up at 4pm. They went bowling, to the movies and had dinner in his hotel room. They had sex all night until it was time to take him to the airport at 7 am in the morning. They arrived at the airport.

"Well I am going to miss you, Brandon. When are you coming back?" Chelsea said putting the car into park.

"I told you I might come back next weekend. I am not for sure yet. I know you work a tight schedule so I would say whenever you were in Atlanta come by the campus or text me. I say it will be better to come by my job, because we are beginning training camp. Also you know I will be with my wife."

"I know baby, but I am going to miss you. You are a good man and have some good ass dick," Chelsea said having a flashback.

Brandon leaned over to give her a kiss. "Trust me, I will be back to give you this dick. I will call you when I land. Okay baby?"

"Yes baby," she said giving him a hug.

He opened the door to get out and opened the trunk. He started to walk off and looked back and blew her a kiss. She waved bye and drove off. He took his phone out and started to make a call going into the airport. His flight wasn't until another hour so Brandon just got something to eat and stayed on his phone texting and he called his wife.

The next hour it was time to load up on the airplane and head to Atlanta. Brandon slept mostly on the plane. He saw a white flight attendant that was showing interest but he had too much on his plate. When Brandon landed in Atlanta he turned his phone off of airplane mode. He got two texts from Chelsea.

"I am missing you already. My room smells like you. I have to see you next week even if I have to get a ticket to come there or get you a ticket to come here. I hope you land safely. Please call me when you land baby."

The next text read. "I know your flight didn't take that long. You know we won't be able to talk unless you get in touch with me. Please call or text me back. I am missing you."

Brandon ignored it and started to call his wife. He wasn't worried about Chelsea anymore. He got what he wanted from her and didn't worry about calling her. He knew she wouldn't come to the school to see him, because of campus security. Brandon was happy to get his rocks off. He grabbed his duffle bag, got off of the plane and headed to his car. He knew had an emotional day with his wife ahead of him.

Chapter Six

Leave Your Wife, Brandon

Brandon made sure he was by his wife side during the bad news over the weekend. Brandon celebrated his birthday with his wife at home. That evening they went out for dinner and tried to make a baby. Chelsea texted him all day on his birthday letting him know she was going to be his birthday present. Brandon never texted back. He blocked Chelsea's number after she kept texting his phone for the next couple of days. He was glad that his wife doesn't check his phone. Thursday morning Brandon's training camp began. He couldn't wait for the season to start and knew they had a great team that could get to the championship game. It was 94 degrees and the players didn't care how hot it was. They were ecstatic about the talent on the team. Their work ethnic was good enough to get to the National Championship game. One of the young white counselors that was Brandon's close friend walked on the field calling Brandon's name.

"Brandon! Brandon!" he said shaking the head coach's hand.

Brandon walked over to Tim the counselor. "What's up Tim?"

"Hey buddy, I came over here to let you know you had a visitor.

"Oh yeah, who is it? Is it that player from Killen Texas?" Brandon smiled thinking he had another star coming to the school.

Tim signaled for Brandon to walk over away from the team.

"No, it is a woman man. Now listen, your wife knows my wife man. What the hell are you doing?"

"Tim....calm...down....you are overacting right now. It is probably a mother of one of the players. "

Tim shook his head. "No it isn't. Her name is Chelsea."

Brandon's head went to the side with his hand on his hip. "What the fuck Tim? You didn't let her in my office did you?"

"Yeah I did man. I couldn't let her just sit outside of your office."

"How can she be in my office Tim? Shit!"

"Listen, man I didn't know that was the chick you fucked in Houston."

"Yeah it is, but how can she get on campus like that?"

"She's is alumni here. She graduated at the top of her class with a 3.9 GPA"

"How do you know that?"

"She told me. She didn't tell you that?"

"No, I didn't give a damn. I just wanted to fuck her and diss her. I didn't know she would really come to my job. What does she have on?" Brandon said waving his finger to the head coach and walking towards his office.

"Man she is fine ass fuck!"

"I know that, but what does she have on?"

She has on this tight cherry dress and cherry heels. The dress is so little where you can see her panties every time she walks. She smells good and her hair is......"

"Okay, thank you Tim. Man fuck man. How can she get on campus wearing that?"

"When campus police saw her they probably was like fuck it. She is too fine."

"Damn man!"

"I thought you blocked her and etc."

"Shit, I did. Fuck man this bitch is going to give me problems. I knew she was crazy but not like this to come to my job."

"How did she find you?"

"I told her I work here."

Tim stopped Brandon with his hand on his shoulder. "Dude, why? We have gone over this so much. We do not tell these bitches where we work. We do not tell them our real names. What the fuck is wrong with you?"

"Man she is sexy as hell and a flight attendant. She is like one of the baddest bitches I ever fucked. Her eyes are sexy as hell. I got caught up in all of that. I don't know what I was thinking plus the pussy is so good."

"I understand dude, good ass pussy comes from crazy ass women. You need to always remember that. You don't really know anything really about her. You better protect yourself. If she popped up at your job just imagine what she is capable of doing."

"I got this," he said walking into the building heading to his office. "I will see you later" Brandon said with his hand on the knob walking in.

He looked at Chelsea bent over showing her ass. She looked over her right shoulder with her finger in her mouth.

"So your wife just called your office phone and left a message on how sorry she is that she cannot give you a baby," she said pulling her skirt to her stomach. She began shaking her ass. She placed her hands on the desk.

"Don't say anything at all. I want you to fill me up with that fat ass dick now! I told you I was going to be your birthday present."

Brandon wanted to know why she was at his job but couldn't resist her. He pulled his black shorts down. He threw his team visor hat on the floor and jacked his dick until he was semi hard to slide in. Chelsea looked back at him and grabbed his shirt.

"I am not going to ask you again. Fuck me. Fuck this birthday pussy," she said looking into his eyes with fierceness waiting to get fucked.

Brandon slid in with 8 inches up and felt her wetness.

"That is a good boy. Fuck that dick feels so good. I want that dick all the way hard. You feel so fucking good right now."

"Shhh...I need you to hush for a minute. No one can know you are here."

"Make me be quiet nigga!" Chelsea said loudly.

Brandon placed his hands over her mouth and started to pound her pussy. He was paranoid but didn't think about it anymore after each stroke. He watched her ass bounce off of him. He fucked her ten minutes until he had to nut.

"Oh my God this pussy is so good," he said whispering in her ear. "I have to cum," he said removing his hand from her mouth.

She moaned softly. "Are you enjoying your birthday pussy?"

"Hell yeah."

"You like the way that pussy feels?"

"Hell yeah I do."

"Good boy, momma wants you to cum in her mouth."

Brandon slid out and jacked his dick. Chelsea got down and caught his nut on her tongue and swallowed his cum. His knees buckled and he couldn't move. She sucked his balls and sucked all the cum out of him. He pulled his shorts up and buttoned them up. Chelsea wiped the cum from the side of her mouth and sat down in the leather chair. Brandon walked over grabbing a water out of his little black refrigerator.

"Do you want a water?"

"I am good. I just had some protein," she said smiling.

Brandon couldn't help that lust was there. He wanted her to leave but she was too sexy.

"Why are you here?" he asked drinking his water.

"I get it. I know you can't call because you are at home with your wife. I get it. I wanted to let you know that I missed you. I am going to be off for today and I got a room at the Sleepless Inn downtown. I wanted to see you again and get fucked. What is wrong with that?"

"You are at my job. You can't just pop up and come to my job. My wife sometimes comes to my job. Luckily it was Tim that brought you to my office because if it was anyone else they probably would've told my wife. You have to respect my life."

"I do respect. Trust me I do, but you have to understand what we did last weekend. It was great. You gave me some good ass dick. I needed it again. Is that too much to ask for? I told you I was going to be your birthday pussy. I made that promise to you," she said spreading her legs showing her pussy with no panties on.

"Fuck you are so amazing. I cannot believe I am fuckin you."

"Brandon, I need you to leave your wife and be mine. Whenever you are ready to leave her understand that I will be loyal to you. I want you to understand that I will be number two until I am number one. I want to give you a baby," she said standing up and leaning over the desk.

"Shit…that hair…your eyes," he said getting aroused.

"Tonight, I want you to cum in this pussy. Are you going to cum in my pussy tonight?"

"Hell yes, I am."

"Are you going to leave your wife to be with me?"

"I am going to leave her," Brandon said hypnotized.

"You want some more of this pussy?"

"I do," he said standing up and walking over.

She turned around as he walked over towards her. She got down slowly and back up.

"You can have some more of this pussy tonight. I will be waiting for you. I am in room 203. I am headed there now. I will see you at 7pm not a minute late. I will have dinner prepared, so be there.

Brandon thought about Bible study with his wife but knew he had to get out of it for Chelsea.

"I have Bible study tonight and it might be after that."

"Oh no, I know. She said that Darren was speaking at 6 not 6:30. But from the sound of it she likes him. Like I said I will see you tonight." She pulled her dress down and walked towards the door.

"How do you know that?"

"Trust me, honey a woman knows everything. "

"Damn that is crazy," he said thinking if Darren and his wife had anything going on. "You want me to walk you out?"

"Remember no one knows I am here. Trust me you are the only one getting this pussy. You don't have to worry about no one getting me boo. Tonight we are making a baby," she said walking out. Brandon stood there with an erection knowing that he didn't want to make a baby, but Chelsea was too sexy to pass up on. He was going to skip Bible study for lust. The night where all hell was going to break loose.

Chapter Seven
Atlanta to Houston

Later in the day Brandon came home and Vanessa was there cooking. He walked in the kitchen.

"Hey baby, how was your day?" she asked stirring the stainless pot and getting a kiss on the cheek from Brandon.

"It was good. Listen, I won't be able to go to Bible study tonight."

She turned around watching him sit on the kitchen counter. "Why?"

"I have a late meeting tonight."

"But baby, tonight Darren was teaching class. The pastor gave him control tonight. I really want us to support him."

"You like Darren don't you?" he asked jumping off the counter.

"Where the hell is that coming from?"

"That is the reason why we go to this church now isn't it?"

"Brandon, you are tripping right now and you better cool it."

"No, you listen to me. I know you have a thing for Darren. You can come clean."

"He has been a family friend for twelve years now. You know he used to be married to my cousin Stacy."

"I know you like him."

"You know what. I am going to finish cooking, because you are tripping right now." She turned around checking her food.

"You are going to disrespect me in my own house?" he asked balling his fist up.

"Nigga, who you think you are talking to?" she asked turning around. "Oh so you want to hit me now? Go ahead...I wish you would," she said throwing the spoon on the stove.

"You do not talk to me any kind of way in my house do you hear me?"

"Nigga, go ahead and hit me. I am tired of you always accusing me of cheating. Are you cheating on me?

Someone who keeps accusing someone of cheating is cheating. Are you cheating?"

"Man no one is accusing you of cheating. I just asked you a question."

"And now I am asking you a question. Are you cheating on me?"

"I am going to go take a shower. I don't have time to hear this shit right now," he said walking off.

"Are you cheating Brandon? Huh? Are you going to wash the bitch pussy juices off of your dick?" she shouted throwing a fit.

Brandon stopped halfway to the stairs rail. He thought she knew but called her bluff. He turned around and walked back to the kitchen.

"So you think I was fucking another woman instead of doing my job at work? You want to get on your knees and smell my sweaty balls. Go ahead. I don't have a damn thing to hide from you."

Vanessa started to get emotional and coming to hug him. "Oh baby, I am so sorry. I am just emotional because I won't be able to…"

"Hey, what did I tell you about talking negative?" he asked kissing her. "I know baby and I am so sorry for thinking you had a thing for Darren.

"It is okay baby, go ahead and take your shower dinner will be ready when you get done. Brandon gave her a hug and a kiss and went upstairs. He knew that was a close call and got out his phone and started to text Chelsea. He knew he had blocked her but couldn't beat the lust he was having for her. He walked in the bedroom and took off his shoes and walked into the bathroom to run the shower.

He texted her. "Hey, where are you?"

She texted him back instantly. "I am at the mall getting something."

"Did you wear that skirt to the mall?"

"Yes."

Brandon got upset and called her.

She picked up. "Hello."

"Why did you wear that skirt there?" Brandon asked lowly with authority.

"Whoa. I told you this was your pussy. I didn't feel like going back to the room yet. I wanted to come to the mall and get something. What is wrong?"

"I don't want anyone to see you in that. You are looking too damn good," he said wanting to ask if any men hit on her.

"Listen Brandon.....hey, I am fine," she said speaking to a guy that told her she was looking sexy.

"Who was that?"

"Some guy telling me I am looking sexy, but like I was telling you, I am..."

"Chelsea, I need you to leave the mall and go to the room. I will be there at 6:30."

"But baby, I wanted to get..."

"Leave Chelsea," he said looking to see if his wife was coming.

"What time is she going to Bible study?"

"In an hour. It starts at 6, but I need you to leave now."

"I don't understand. I am not going to give this pussy away and I am number two right now."

"You will be my wife and have my child, but I need you to leave okay?"

"Okay, baby, I am going to leave and go to the room to prepare for us."

"Okay great," he said taking his clothes off. "I will see you in a bit."

"Okay babe," she said hanging up the phone.

Brandon walked in the shower and started to think about everything he was doing wrong. He loved his wife but he had lust for Chelsea. His phone vibrated. He thought that might have been Chelsea. He wiped his face from all the water that was running down his face.

He reached out of the shower to the white space saver which was over the toilet storage unit. Vanessa grabbed his hands as he opened his eyes.

"Dinner is served," she said walking into the shower. She placed her elbows against the shower wall shaking her ass.

"I have been a bad girl. I need you to fuck me right now."

Brandon didn't want to because he had fucked Chelsea and had to fuck in a couple of hours. His dick got hard and he fucked her. They made love twenty minutes in the shower and she walked out to the bedroom to get ready for Bible study and dinner. Brandon was trying to catch his breath. He turned the shower off to check to see who had either called or texted him. He stepped out and looked at his phone. It was a text message and he just smiled. Brandon went and texted Chelsea to let her know that his wife was going to leave soon. Brandon got ready to see her and for dinner as well.

He put on black sweatpants, a black V-neck shirt and flip-flops. He went downstairs. He went to the table and they started to eat. After they finished eating his wife left to go to Bible study. Brandon walked her out and went upstairs to spray on some cologne. When he sprayed the cologne on himself, the doorbell rang. Brandon didn't know who it was so he went downstairs. When he opened the door it was Chelsea. Brandon was angry and hoping his wife didn't see her. He grabbed her by the right hand and brought her in the house.

"What the fuck are you doing here?" Brandon asked closing the door hard.

She dropped her black trench coat off and threw it on the floor. She wore pink panties and took them off and threw them on the ground. Brandon couldn't beat the lust he felt for her. She walked to him while he talked.

"My wife could have seen you. How the fuck did you know where I lived?"

She bent down and pulled his pants around his ass to let his dick fall out. She began sucking his dick. Brandon stopped talking and started to moan. She slobbed on his dick while he gripped her ass. He took his shirt off and threw it on the floor.

"Every time I get mad at you….you find some way to make me shut the fuck up."

She muffled yes with his dick in her mouth.

"Come fuck me in y'all bedroom."

"You know I can't do that. She will smell your perfume. I would have to wash the sheets and etc. Let's go to your hotel. She will be back in an hour."

"She took her pink heels off and threw them to the side and started to walk to the stairs.

"I know it is this way so I will see you when you get up there."

Brandon just looked at her with a big fat dick ready to get some pussy. He knew what he was about to do was wrong but he couldn't fight it. He got naked and followed her. When he got up the stairs he saw her on the edge of the bed playing with her pussy. Brandon held his dick in his hand and closed the door to go fuck her.

Brandon fucked her for thirty minutes and did exactly what he said he was going to do and that was to cum in her. He didn't want to do it but she was so sexy and her pussy was so good to him. He looked at the clock and told her she had to leave. They went downstairs to get dressed and Chelsea gave him a hug.

She left and Brandon went to the kitchen to spray it with smell good before his wife came. He went to pull the sheets and get every scent out the house of Chelsea. After forty minutes his wife came home. Brandon made it just in time where he couldn't get caught.

"You must didn't go to your meeting?"

"Naw they canceled it at the last minute, so since you weren't feeling well I went ahead and cleaned up a little bit for you."

She hugged him and thanked him. "Thank you baby. I am going to get ready to watch my shows. I have to be at work very early tomorrow. I have a couple of patients that are having a baby."

"I will be up there in a minute baby. I am going to watch a little sport tonight.

She gave him a kiss and he waited for her to go upstairs to see if he was going to get caught. He waited for about ten minutes and it was nothing but the TV. He knew he was home free. He had to watch out for Chelsea because she was getting crazy every minute and every day. He turned the TV up and called Chelsea.

"Hello?"

"Chelsea, please tell me how you knew where I lived?" he asked whispering.

"Are you coming baby?"

"My wife is here now. I told her the meeting was canceled. There is no way I can come tonight."

"You fuckin' lied to me!"

"Calm down. I could have stayed out late if you would have never come here, but answer me how did you know where I stayed?"

Brandon heard a woman in the background.

"Who is that?" Brandon asked sitting up.

"Star, he talking about he might not come?"

"Who the fuck is Star?"

"She is a girl I met at the mall. I was getting this nice lingerie set for you today and we bumped into each other. She was telling me how sexy I looked and I told her the same thing. I told her that my man birthday was Tuesday and asked would she do a threesome. She agreed and now she is here waiting on you naked. She is like 6'5, Amazon, thick as hell, big ass tits and booty. She is brown skin like me with long Brazilian hair and a nose piercing. If you don't come I am just going to let her eat my pussy and spend the night with me. I know I told you no one would get this pussy but I meant a man. She is too bad to send home. I was going to watch her suck your dick and fuck you. I showed her a picture of you and told her you were the defensive coordinator for Georgia Tech."

Brandon stood up in disbelief. He couldn't believe everything Chelsea was saying at one time.

"Wait...hold on slow your damn roll. I have so many questions to ask you."

"Okay, Star. I am going to step outside real quick."

"Is he coming?" Star asked Chelsea.

"I don't know yet. I will let you know in a minute" she walked out of the room. 'What's up?"

"First, why didn't you let me know you were trying to have a threesome? I could have come there instead of here."

"It was supposed to be a surprise baby. Do you want to see a picture of her?"

"No....and right there. How did you get a picture of me? I never sent you one."

"From the video camera silly. I never erased the video."

Brandon was upset. "Wait. I thought I told you to erase it?"

"Well from the great weekend we had we both forgot to erase it. I was like well I am going to keep it and look at it to see that long dick in my pussy."

"Chelsea, I need you to erase that picture and that video immediately."

"Your mind shouldn't be on any picture or videos right now. It should be over here with me and Star. Now what you need to do is bring your ass over here and get some pussy."

"I told you I cannot just leave like that. Okay? How do you know where I live?"

"I mean what is this 21 question day? Shit!"

"Tell me how did you find out!"

"Well remember when I was in your office I went through your desk and got all your information. I also took a picture naked in your chair holding the picture of you and your wife."

Brandon wanted to shout. "Chelsea! What the fuck? Are you crazy?"

"I am crazy in love with you."

"How can you be in love with me after a week?"

"You are sexy. You have a big dick. You spent time with me. I mean you are a good man."

"Chelsea, you do understand I cannot leave my wife. If I get caught she will almost take everything from me."

"I don't give a fuck. You told me she isn't getting a dime. You must think you are messing with a dumb ass bitch. Nigga I had a 3.9 GPA."

"Fuck man. Listen, I can't come okay but I can meet you in the morning. What time does your plane leave?"

"It is at 10am."

"I can meet you at your hotel 7 am."

"Hold on," she said opening up the door. "Star, what time you have class?"

"At 8. Why?"

"He said he won't be here until 7."

"I will stay until he gets here then."

"Okay," she said closing the door. "That is cool. She said she will wait for you. I guess I will see you in the morning. I can't wait to give you your present. You are going to enjoy it."

"I can't wait either," Brandon said excited over the phone but really scared.

"I will see you in the morning baby."

"One more thing. You can't keep telling everyone where I work at. I am kind of known and I am married."

"Bye Brandon," Chelsea said hanging up the phone.

Brandon knew he shouldn't have fucked Chelsea but her sexiness got him. The house phone rung and Brandon got nervous. He heard Vanessa pick it up. Brandon rushed upstairs to the bedroom.

"Oh no, it is okay," Vanessa said hanging up the phone.

He swallowed. "Who was that?"

"Wrong number. Someone calling from a hotel looking for Star. Sounds like she was looking for a stripper." Vanessa laughed. "What is wrong with you?" Vanessa asked looking back at the TV screen.

"Nothing I am about to use the bathroom." Brandon went into the bathroom and his phone vibrated. It was text message from Chelsea. He opened it and it was Star eating Chelsea's pussy. Brandon dropped the phone. He wanted to leave but had to wait until the morning. He texted her back.

"Why did you call the house phone? Stop messing around here!"

"Bye Brandon. As you can see I am getting my pussy ate. Good night. Go to your wife but you will be with your side chick in the morning giving you a late birthday present."

Brandon didn't text back. He was scared of Chelsea. He knew had to play her game. She had so much blackmail on him that he was going to do anything she wanted in order to keep her from saying something to his wife.

The next day in the morning Brandon went over to her hotel and fucked Star and Chelsea. Chelsea kicked Star out after ten minutes of fucking because he was fucking her too well. Brandon didn't know what to expect with this chick. He knew she was going to give him more than he can handle. They fucked until she had to leave and he went to work scared out of his mind.

He knew what he had done was a mistake. He loved his wife but was done with her. He didn't want Chelsea but couldn't fight the lust.

Chapter Eight
Kind of Tired of This

A couple of months later everything with Brandon and Vanessa was going well. Their chemistry was getting better. It was opening day for Georgia Central Flyers September 12, 2012. Chelsea and Brandon spent more time together as well. Chelsea came to visit Brandon very often. He even flew to be with her on her birthday. On opening day before kickoff Chelsea sent Brandon a text. Brandon went into his office and read his text from Chelsea.

The text read, "Brandon, good luck on your game today baby. I just wanted to let you know that I went to the doctor today.

I know I didn't tell you but I am three months as of today. Congrats baby. Please get back at me when the game is over."

Brandon dropped his phone with Vanessa walking in the office. Brandon quickly picked his phone up.

"Hey baby, I know the game begins in a bit but I wanted to come give you some sugar."

Brandon was startled. "Hey baby" he walked over giving her a hug and kiss putting his phone in his pocket.

"Your family and I will be sitting together. I saw them when I got here, so I am going to sit with them. Are you okay?"

"Oh yeah baby. I am just kind of nervous and excited at the same time. You scared me. I need to get my guys together."

"Okay, baby, listen are we going to that Chinese spot later tonight to celebrate our nine year anniversary?"

"Yeah baby, you know we got too. Our nine years of hell," he said laughing and walking her to the door.

"Anyway....good luck baby. I will see you after the game" she kissed him and left.

Brandon closed the door and grabbed his phone to call Chelsea. The phone rang one time and went to voicemail. He called three times after that and it went straight to voicemail. He figured she was at work.

"Coach. We are about to go out to the field," one of the coaches said opening the door.

"Okay, I am about to come now."

The coach closed the door and Brandon left a voicemail.

"Chelsea, now look, we cannot have a baby right now, okay. First of all, both of our careers are taken off. You just got a raise and the season is starting for me. Besides, baby, I want to do this right with you. I want to be married to you first. I love you, Chelsea and I want to make sure the baby have his parents together not separated. So baby, please get an abortion. I told you. I am trying to get that job out there at Dallas so we can be together baby. I want to be married to you first.

If I don't answer my phone it's because the game is about to start. I love you, Chelsea, baby. It doesn't matter how much it will cost just let me know so I can forward the money to your account. Love you, bye." Brandon hung up and placed his phone into the drawer. He closed it and walked out the door, locked it, and prepared for the game.

Three hours later Georgia Central Flyers lost by three. They still were happy because the team they faced was ranked number #10. The fact that Georgia Central Flyers was ranked #25 made them feel good. They were confident about their team. The team huddled up in the locker room and the coaches gave their speeches. It was Brandon's turn to say words to the team but all he could think of was Chelsea. He hoped she was going to think twice about the baby and have an abortion.

He gave his speech and the team huddled together to put their hands in and yelled "Flyers!" Brandon walked off and went into his office. He walked in and his wife was in his office.

"Good game baby. I am so proud of you guys. You guys gave it all you got," Vanessa said hugging and kissing Brandon.

Brandon was scared and hesitant. "Hey baby, thank you so much. How did you get in here?"

"Brandon, really? You've been gave me a key. I have a key to everything honey."

"Oh yeah. I am tripping right now. I am sorry."

"Well I know you have to take a shower and everything. Oh just remember our reservation is at nine. It is 6:45 pm now. I am going to go to my cousin

Tammy's house to see her new baby. I will meet you there."

"Okay, baby, I will see you in a bit. I love you," Brandon said kissing her and walking her to the door.

"I love you too" she gave him a kiss and walked out.

Brandon quickly turned around and went into his drawer. He got his phone and saw the light on his phone go off. He saw a voicemail. He quickly checked his voicemail and it was Chelsea. Chelsea talking kind of sadly said, "Are you serious right now?

I am so happy that I am going to have your child and you want to kill it? Why Brandon? You know what? If that's what going to make you happy I will get the abortion. I agree with the decision of us being married and us having a child. That is the way I wanted to do it. I will set something up on my off day Monday or Tuesday. I forgot to tell you I am off those days. I am not going to come this time. I am kind of tired of traveling there and working. I am going to relax. I know it is your anniversary. I am going to let you enjoy your last one with her. I can't wait for ours baby. You need to stop looking for that job in Dallas because I am pretty sure Houston has some spots open as well. I will talk to you later baby."

Brandon blew and said. "Thank God but she is kind of crazy. She will lie to me. I have to call her." Brandon got his things and walked out of the office to get in his car. He was greeted by coaches and players. He spoke to them and made his way to his car. Soon as he got into his car his phone rang. It was Chelsea. He picked up.

"Hello?" Brandon sounded worried.

"Hey babe," Chelsea sounded sad.

"What is wrong?"

"I am going to kill our baby."

"But baby, I told you why…"

"I know but I know we will have a gorgeous baby. I don't want to kill it but I do want to do it right. I don't know what I was thinking a couple of months ago. I should have listened and not let you get me pregnant. I am so sorry baby."

"It is okay baby. You are just in love with me that's all. Are you done with work?"

"No, I just got back to Houston. I go to Phoenix in a little bit. The plane leaves in thirty minutes. Go enjoy your anniversary. Hey, what are you going to do for New Years? I know you have to spend time with her on the other holidays."

"Well my plan would be a bowl game. If not I don't have anything, but I am planning to be at a bowl game."

"Did you want me to come?"

"Ummm…well you know my wife would be there."

"But baby, you told me going into the New Year it would be over."

"I told you that I am trying to get a job out there first before anything. You have to work with me baby."

"But why are you trying to go to Dallas for? Why not come out here with me? Don't you want to be closer to me baby?"

"I do but they pay more in Dallas. It is a great opportunity for me. Plus you can apply at the airport in Dallas. Come on now. We have talked about this. I thought we were going to stick to this plan."

"Yeah, but I really don't want to be that far from my mom, if you are serious about us, I will do it."

"Thanks baby, if it is a great job that comes up in Houston, I will apply for it.

I want to make you happy. I know you don't want to be that far from your mom, so I will fill out an application if a job comes up. I love you."

"Thank you baby." Chelsea got a little excited. "I got to go. I love you baby."

"I love you too. I can't wait to see you again. You know when I get time to come out there I will come out there. I will talk to you later." They hung up. Brandon drove to his house to get ready for his anniversary dinner with his wife.

Their anniversary dinner went well. Vanessa and Brandon were happy. They spent all the holidays together. Chelsea had the abortion and was happy she got to see Brandon twice a month. However, it wasn't enough because she was in love with him and wanted more time.

She was getting frustrated not seeing the man she loved. She paid attention to his team's record to see if they were going to make a bowl. They did so Chelsea knew that she wouldn't bring the New Year in with him. Three months later everything was going well for Brandon. He balanced his marriage and side chick's relationship. The team made a bowl game and played on New Year's Day at the Georgia Dome. Chelsea flew into town on New Year's Eve without letting Brandon know.

She was trying to get some type of time with him. She let him know she was in town and wanted to bring the New Year in with him. Brandon let her know that he normally spend New Year's Day at church. Chelsea let Brandon know that if she didn't get to bring New Year's in with him that she was going to let his wife know about her dealings with him.

Brandon had so much on his plate already and she was stressing him out. Chelsea settled into her hotel at 4 pm. She called Brandon. He didn't pick up. Minutes later, he called back.

She picked up, "Hey baby, where have you been? I have been trying to get in touch with you."

"I have been with the team. We have a big game tomorrow."

"I know you guys are going to win."

"Thank you. Where are you?"

"I am here."

"Here where?" Brandon asked sitting up in his leather chair in his office.

"I am in Atlanta."

"What are you doing here?"

"I am going to the game. I'd been got my ticket and hotel. I wanted to surprise you."

"Chelsea, you know my wife will be there."

"Shut up!" she yelled. "I am so fucking sick of you talking about your wife. I am your Goddamn wife. I told you if you keep stringing me along like this I am going to end your marriage myself. I saw a job opening in Houston that pays more than Dallas. I'll forward the information to your email."

"How the fuck did you get my email? I never gave it to you."

"Your office and don't curse at me either. Now look, are you going to spend time with me or not?"

"I told you I go to church on New Year's Eve. I can come after then."

"Fuck coming after, tell me where the church is and I will come."

"I am not going to tell you where I go to church. Are you crazy? My wife will be there."

"What the fuck did I just tell you?!" she shouted. "You know what…okay fine Brandon. I will wait for you tonight. I will go out and have a little fun."

"Where do you think you are going?"

"Go be with your wife." Chelsea hung up the phone.

Brandon was getting tired of her crap. He wished many times he would have never met her. He finished everything and walked out of his office. Later that night Brandon and Vanessa went to church to bring the New Year's in. With 15 minutes remaining to bring in 2013 Brandon was singing a gospel song. The church was full and they sat in the very back. Brandon turned to the left to see everyone who was coming in. He saw Chelsea walking in.

It seemed like the world stopped. Brandon stopped singing. Chelsea smiling walked in and sat on the left side of the church.

She wore a baby blue dress to her knees and blue heels. Many of the men in church looked at her. Vanessa looked at Brandon.

"Baby, what are you looking at?"

"I thought that Sister Trish was coming back to our church."

"Oh no, baby, I don't know who she is," Vanessa said as she started back singing.

The song was over and the pastor was up talking. Brandon kept turning to the side looking at Chelsea. She didn't look his way.

The New Year came in and everyone shouted and hugged each other. Brandon saw Chelsea hugging one of the guys at church. He got jealous and looked at her and whispered, "Stop it."

Vanessa saw him and said, "What did you just say to her?"

"I wasn't looking at her. I was looking at Brother John hugging her. It just looks like it. I hope he gets her number."

"She looks like a little plastic doll slut. I am going to talk to her after church and see what she is all about."

"What? Why?"

"You know I am nosey baby."

Minutes later church was over. Everyone started to hug and speak to each other. Some members were walking outside. Vanessa put her black leather jacket on and walked outside following Chelsea.

Brandon got scared and walked out not finishing his conversation with one of the deacons. He went outside in the cold early morning air. He saw his wife and Chelsea talking. He walked over.

"Hey baby," Vanessa said telling Brandon to come over. "This is Chelsea. She just moved to Atlanta last week and looking for a church. She graduated from Georgia Central as well. She was a freshman when I was a junior and you were a senior. She remembers when you played football because she was a cheerleader. That is probably where you remember her from."

"Oh yeah. I remember you now," Brandon said playing it off.

"You were very good. I remember when you had four sacks in your third game as a senior. You were a beast," she said shaking her hand.

"Thank you."

"Sister Vanessa, Deacon Darren wants you," Sister Pam said shouting her name.

"It was good meeting you, Chelsea," Vanessa said shaking her hand.

"Nice meeting you too."

"Baby, I will be back." She gave him a kiss and walked into church.

"Okay baby. Chelsea what the hell are you doing here? How did you know where I was?"

"I followed you guys here. She is going to see Darren. How does that make you feel?"

"Shut up. Enough is enough. Your little game is over. You are pushing it."

"No you are pushing it. I have so much on you Brandon and I am tired of your little games. I am going to be your new wife and you need to get that through your head."

"I told you I cannot leave her until I hear something. You are going to mess everything up."

"What am I going to mess up?"

"Me having a job and a place to stay."

"You can come stay with me. I told you about looking at jobs in Houston. You have someone to stay with baby."

"Stop it. Okay….I will look at jobs after the game. Please give me some time baby."

"Okay, I will. Are you still coming over?"

"I told you yes. I will come up with something, but now you have to leave."

"Okay, baby. I will see you soon. It is too cold out here." Chelsea backed up and winked her eyes at Brandon and walked to her car.

Vanessa walked back outside. "Is she gone?"

"Yeah," he said giving her a hug.

"Good, because she looks crazy. I didn't like how she was looking at you. Stay away from her. It is time to go. I am ready to go drink and have a little time for us. Let's go celebrate the New Year baby."

Brandon and Vanessa got in the car and went home. Brandon knew he couldn't tell his wife that he couldn't spend time with her. He knew he was in trouble either way. What he didn't know is Chelsea had other plans for him.

Chapter Nine
I'm Going to Kill Her

Brandon texted Chelsea to let her know he wouldn't be able to come. Chelsea told him it was okay and she wasn't mad. She would go support him for his game. Brandon knew something was wrong because she didn't trip. So many things went through his head. Did she have one of the guys from church there? Was she going to tell his wife the truth? Brandon didn't know what to expect. He had a great night of pleasure with his wife. The next day it was game day.

Brandon still didn't hear anything from Chelsea from the morning to the afternoon. He called and she didn't pick up.

The game started at 8pm and the team was at the Georgia Dome preparing. Still nothing from her. He guessed Chelsea gave up on them but he was still worried. She texted him before the team went out on the field before the game.

Chelsea texted him, "I had a little way too much to drink last night. I got a bottle last night and passed out. I leave in the morning and I hope you will come see me tonight after the game. I am not going to come because I don't want to see her and be out in the cold weather like that."

Brandon was happy and he texted her back. "I understand and I will see you tonight baby."

Brandon and his team went to the field to play and they were 35-14. Everyone was happy and Brandon as well. Brandon had a feeling the way his defense play that he would be able to get the job he wanted. The president and coach from the team in Dallas approached him after the game and told him that they wanted to meet him tomorrow to discuss a contract. They let him know that they were going to fly him there 7 in the morning on Tuesday. Brandon was happy and finally his dreams were coming true. After the meeting, Brandon sent two messages letting them know he got the job in Dallas. He didn't tell his wife or Chelsea either. Chelsea called his phone.

"Congrats baby! Your defense was on it tonight. I am so happy for you."

"Thank you so much baby. Hey, I feel like celebrating tonight. My wife is going to hang out with her cousin's tonight. She isn't coming home. Do you want to come over and spend the night with me?"

Chelsea got happy. "Yes, baby. When are you going home?"

"I will be there at 1, but check this out I have an extra key underneath the mat. Use it and be naked waiting for me on the bed. I can't wait to come home to some good ass pussy."

"Yes, baby…let me go ahead and get ready now. I love you."

"I love you too. "

They hung up the phone. Vanessa walked into his office to celebrate his victory. She told him that she was going to her cousin's house to drink. He didn't tell her about his job offer.

After the finished their conversation Brandon rushed home. He walked in and heard music was playing. He smiled and walked up to the stairs. He opened the door and the lights were on. Chelsea lay in the middle of the bed naked playing with her pussy. Brandon walked up to her. Getting in the bed he started to eat her pussy. He teased her and stopped.

"Baby." Brandon stopped tasting her. "Listen, I have something to tell you."

"Why now baby? Damn, your tongue was feeling good. What is it?" she asked sitting up naked fixing her hair.

"I got the job in Houston baby. I leave in the morning at 10."

Chelsea jumped up and down on the bed with excitement. "Yay baby, we can be together now."

"I know right. I am so excited. I get to be close to you, but I won't be able to get there until the summer. Here is the thing though. My wife is going to have to go unless…"

"Unless what baby?"

"Let's go take a shower. I will tell you while I am fucking you," he said getting out of the bed grabbing her hand.

They rushed into the bathroom and took a shower. They fucked each other until the morning. Chelsea had to leave early to go to her room to leave to go back to Houston and Brandon left as well to fly to Dallas.

Brandon let his wife know that he was going to be with the team all day to celebrate and get ready for the festivities. She let him know that she had to work and wouldn't be able to come to any of the festivities. He knew she had to work and his plan was going well.

A couple months later in May, Chelsea was ready for Brandon to move to Houston. Vanessa still had no clue about Brandon and his new job. He had put in his two weeks' notice before school was out. Brandon was going to start his new job June 22nd.

Chelsea wanted to let Vanessa know she had won. She had her house on the market ready for sale. Brandon told her that they would move in together. He didn't know she was ready to sell her house. One early Tuesday morning on May 14, 2013 Chelsea called the house phone. She knew Brandon was at work. She was hoping Vanessa was at home. The phone rang and Vanessa picked up.

"Hello," Vanessa said ready to walk out of the door to head to talk.

"Hey, is this Vanessa?" Chelsea asked blocking her number.

"Yes, this is. Who is this?

"It doesn't matter who this is. I want to let you know that your husband will be my husband soon."

She laughed. "Bitch what is you talking about?"

"You want to laugh at me huh? It won't be funny once he leaves you."

Vanessa tried to figure out her voice. "Again, bitch, who is this?"

"Listen, bitch!!! You must don't know about me and him. You must don't know that he got a job here at the Houston Texans facility. I wanted to let you know I'm his new wife, so once he gives you those divorce papers just be a good girl and sign them.

"Bitch, first of all he isn't going anywhere. Brandon loves me. Secondly, I don't know anything about him getting a job in Houston. I know he is going to Houston for someone signing day. Bitch is this Chelsea?"

She clapped her hands. "Good for you bitch!!! You finally figured it out. Now since you know....sign those papers and leave us alone. He is going to give you those divorce papers and then he and I will get married. He is my man. I got to go to work."

"Bitch, I knew you were a slut. Where do you live?"

"I live in Houston. I've been known about you. When your man came to sign their running back I fucked him then." She laughed. "He told me about when you couldn't have a baby and Darren. I know you like Darren. Especially the way you went into the church smiling when he wanted you."

"Bitch you don't know nothing. You better shut the fuck up!!! I am going to skip work and come beat your ass and handle Brandon at the same time."

"Come on to Houston. I have been waiting to beat your ass. My future husband is at Martin Williams High school. Guess I will see you there at three when you get there. Fat bitch!"

Vanessa hung up the phone and called Brandon's phone but no answer. Vanessa called her job to call out and said she had a family emergency. She looked online for plane tickets. She saw a flight at 11 am to Houston. She went to put on blue jeans, solid black tank top, and black and white Jordan's. She booked her flight and headed to the airport.

She called Brandon's phone but still no answer. She printed her ticket from the customer rep and headed to her gate. An hour later it was time for her to get on the plane. She got on the plane and sat towards the middle front of the plane. Chelsea who was on the same flight spotted her. Fire came through her bones.

She knew if Vanessa saw her that she would want to fight. She called Brandon. There was no answer. She hadn't talked to Brandon since last night about him moving with her. She knew he was most likely at work.

She texted him, "Guess what damn it….your wife is aboard this flight. I told her everything. I am going to kill this bitch. I had enough of you giving me shit and this bitch! I have been faithful and just waiting Brandon. I can't wait anymore. You are going to be mine. We just need this bitch out of the way because I don't think she is going to sign those papers. By the time you get this text you better give me an answer at 10:55 pm or I am going to leave her bloody.

"Chelsea we are about to fly in ten minutes get ready girl," one of the flight attendants said.

"Okay." Chelsea called Brandon's phone again. It went straight to voicemail.

"Damn it Brandon five minutes is up. You think I won't? I am going to kill her now or should I leave her bloody? Pick it...you know what? Fuck this talking. I am going right now...good-bye Brandon until I get to our home. Bye."

Chelsea stood up from the back and grabbed an oxygen mask. She started to head towards Vanessa. She slid through the passengers trying to get to their seat. She was behind Vanessa. Vanessa turned around and Chelsea wrapped the string around Vanessa's throat. She started to choke her with it. The passengers got scared. The flight attendants, pilot, and Air Marshall ran to stop Chelsea.

Vanessa tried to grab Chelsea to stop. The Air Marshall grabbed Chelsea's hand to stop her. Vanessa almost passed out until they grabbed her. She coughed trying to catch her breath. The other flight attendants came to her rescue.

"Why didn't you let me kill her? My husband and I need her gone. Please let me kill her" Chelsea yelled. The Air Marshall carried her out the door.

Vanessa caught her breath and wanted to go after Chelsea but was happy she was alive. The flight crew had to go get a nurse to make sure Vanessa was okay. Still no calls to either both of the women from Brandon.

Chapter Ten
The Courtroom of Secrets

Chelsea was quickly arrested and sent to jail. After being nursed Vanessa was okay. After she was done she had to go for questioning at the Atlanta Police Department. She called Brandon and still no answer. After an hour and a half of being at the airport she went home. She saw Brandon's truck in the driveway. She quickly pulled her car in the driveway. She got out and saw boxes in the back of his truck. She walked to the steps. He opened the door having a box of things in his hand. Vanessa wanted answers.

"What the fuck are you doing?" Vanessa said placing her bag on the ground.

Brandon placed the box down. "Vanessa. Hey. I got your calls but I have been packing. I thought you were going to be at work."

"I didn't go because your little slut Chelsea told me you two were supposed to be fucking. Then she told me you got a job in Houston! What the fuck is going on?"

"She told you huh?" Brandon started laughing.

"You think it is very funny?" she said with an attitude.

"She is really crazy."

"I booked a flight to go down there to get in her ass and your ass. I got on this bitch plane not knowing she is a fucking flight attendant! She fucking tried to kill me with an oxygen mask!"

"Damn…she is crazy for real."

"Is all this shit true or what? Did you cheat on me and did you get a job in Houston? She is talking about you got divorce papers. What the fuck is going on?"

Brandon walked back in the house.

"I am talking to you! Did you get a job in Houston?!" She walked in the house leaving the door open.

Brandon went to the living room counter to grab pieces of paper. He handed her the paper and took out a pen.

"Yes, I cheated on you with her and I didn't get a job in Houston. I got a job in Dallas. I start in two weeks. Also I need you to sign these divorce papers. It is over Vanessa. I am leaving you. I do not owe you anything. You can have the house."

Vanessa started to cry. "Are you serious right now?"

"I am leaving," Brandon said walking out of the door.

"Brandon, I am talking to you. Is it because I couldn't have your baby? What is it? I can fix it," Vanessa said following him crying.

Brandon picked up the box and went to his truck. He placed the box in the back with the other boxes and got in.

"I am talking to you. Please baby, talk to me."

Brandon didn't say anything at all. He started up the truck and backed up and left. Vanessa got down on her knees throwing the papers on the ground crying.

****

Vanessa pressed charges against Chelsea. It was her court date to testify against Chelsea. A small courtroom where Vanessa stood next to her lawyer Adam Golden and Chelsea's lawyer Rebecca Williams at the other table. Vanessa wore a long yellow dress with black flats. Vanessa called Brandon before she entered the courtroom four times but he didn't speak up.

The black short chubby bailiff walked in the middle of the courtroom. "ALL RISE!! The Court of General Sessions Forty-Sixth Judicial Circuit is now in session. Judge Steve Rocks is now presiding. Please be seated.

The tall 6'6 old judge with a patch of gray hair walked in to his podium. "Good morning, ladies and gentlemen. Now calling the case of the People of the State of Georgia versus Chelsea Johnson. Are both sides ready?

"Ready for the People, Your Honor," Adam Golden said.

"Ready for the defense, Your Honor," Rebecca Williams said.

Adam Golden let the judge know the charges against Chelsea. Rebecca Williams tried to defend her client. After both statements Vanessa was escorted to the bench. She walked up, was sworn in and sat down. She started to give her testimony or rather sworn statement.

"The next thing I know there was a cord around my throat. I couldn't breathe," Vanessa said almost about to cry.

The court room door opened. It was Brandon walking through the door with Vanessa's cousin Tracy from Dallas. She walked in with her kids and had one on the way. Vanessa locked eyes on them as they came to sit down. Brandon was there to testify next. Vanessa stopped talking as she saw Tracy smile at her.

"What the fuck is this?" Vanessa asked standing up.

"Order! Order!" Judge Rock said. "Miss Daniels, please do not curse in the courtroom and please have a seat."

"So is that who you left me for? You are telling me that is your child?"

They didn't say anything. She watched Brandon put his daughter in the seat and hold his son.

"Hey cousin," Tracy said laughing and waving. "These are all of Brandon's kids," she whispered. Vanessa rushed out from behind the table.

"Bailiff get her now," Judge Rock said standing up banging his gavel.

119

Vanessa went through the double doors and tackled Tracy to the ground. She choked Tracy.

"Get this bitch off of me!" Tracy squirmed to get loose.

The bailiff rushed to pull her off but to no avail. He just couldn't get her off of Tracy. Vanessa reached, unbuckled the bailiff's gun, grabbed it, and...

Prologue Part 2

Tracy locked eyes with Brandon after every stroke he gave her. In and out, 10 ½ inches of dick slid heavily, yet gracefully into Tracy. On top of her, he peeled her left leg towards her stomach and kept her right leg down to scissor fuck her. He inserted himself lying to the right of her, while she gripped his shaved mocha ass.

"You liked how that dick feels?" Brandon asked with sweat dripping from his forehead on to the silk white and baby blue sheets.

"Oh baby, I love how you feel. You fucking this pussy good!" Tracy exclaimed while smacking his ass. He went deeper after every stroke.

"You are going to make me cum all in this pussy."

"Go ahead and do it. Then, you will have a reason to leave Vanessa. You are going to be my man," she gazed into his eyes with love.

"Fuck….tell me to cum inside of you."

"Brandon, cum inside of this pussy and get me pregnant. I want to have your baby."

"I have to cum right now," Brandon said, shooting his load inside of Tracy. He instantly felt weak and laid on top of her. "I never had pussy like that."

"You know, I am very fertile. If you can have kids, then I am pregnant."

"I don't give a fuck. Hopefully, I am going to be a Cowboy next year. Fuck Vanessa!"

"How are you going to get out of that marriage without her getting it all?"

"You let me handle that. I have a plan. I love you baby."

"Brandon, I love you too," Tracy kissed him, while crossing her legs tightly over his ass.

"What is something a man has done wrong to you?"

"Lie to love me."

"Well what is something you want from a man?"

"Stay and love me unconditionally....now fuck me so you can go back to your wife."

Chapter Eleven

She Got Your Gun

Vanessa grabbed the bailiff's gun and Brandon's eyes froze. Both of the lawyers ran out of the courtroom, leaving their briefcases. The judge exited to the backroom quickly. He pulled Tracy back towards the kids to shield him. Tracy's black flats were in the middle of the floor and her dress was wrinkle from the tussle. The kids were crying.

"She got your gun! She has your fucking gun!" Brandon yelled towards the bailiff.

The chubby white bailiff stood on his knees slowly, with Brandon behind him.

"Mrs. Daniels, please drop my gun. Okay, just go ahead and drop the gun. You don't know what you're doing with it," the bailiff pleaded, while reaching for his taser.

Vanessa grabbed his 9 millimeter. She backed up pointing her gun at Brandon and Tracy.

"Throw your taser over here," Vanessa demanded the bailiff.

"Vanessa, what the fuck are you doing?" Brandon asked, with a scold on his face.

"Throw the taser over here now."

The bailiff threw his taser towards Vanessa and she kicked it far, where no one could reach it.

"Shut those kids up", she said with a tight grip on the gun.

"Stop crying babies. Everything is going to be okay, please stop," Tracy said, trying to calm her kids.

The bailiff quietly tried to radio in for back up, while Vanessa was talking. "We have a situation, call the police."

"Why the fuck did you do that? I am trying to make a point. You didn't have to do that," she said getting upset.

"Ma'am, I understand that you are upset right now, but I had to. I have a family and I want to see them. I don't know what your intentions are."

"This has nothing to do with you. It is about this fucking slut and this fucking faggot."

"Please, not in front of the kids. Do not curse in front of my kids," Brandon said with his hands protecting the kids and Tracy.

"Kids? Are you fucking serious right now Brandon? Those are not your fucking kids, Brandon."

"Ma'am, I need you to drop the gun."

"Shut the fuck up. I told you this had nothing to do with you. I need you to shut the fuck up," Vanessa's voice emphatically shook the walls.

"Vanessa, please put the gun down, before you get in trouble or someone gets hurt. You shouldn't have to do all of this. I need you to give the bailiff his gun."

"I am not doing a goddamn thing, Brandon. So, this is who you are leaving me for? You are leaving me for this bitch!" Vanessa yelled, with tears coming down her eyes.

"Who are you calling a bitch?" Tracy said getting furious.

"Bitch, try me," Vanessa said wiping her tears away. "Is this the bitch you are leaving me for?"

The room was silent.

"Answer me, Brandon!" Vanessa said, cocking the gun back.

Everyone's heart started to pound. They got scared, not knowing if Vanessa was going to pull the trigger.

"You know I can shoot Brandon and I won't miss, so bailiff, I do know what the fuck I am doing."

Brandon tried to shield Tracy and the kids with his whole body.

"Vanessa, please put the gun down. This shouldn't have to go this far. Put it down!"

"Miss Vanessa, please put the gun down," the bailiff begged with his hands in the air.

"Didn't I tell your fat ass to shut the fuck up?"

The bailiff talked over her.

"I am not going to shut up. They just radioed in and the police are going to be outside of this courtroom in 45 seconds. They are waiting for you. Ma'am, they will take action, if they have to."

"Let them...I don't care. All I want him to do is answer my fucking questions."

"Vanessa, stop acting like this. You are scaring my kids".

"They are not your kids. Why the fuck are you claiming her kids as yours? Do you think I give a fuck that they are scared? Through all the shit you have put me through, finally I am in control. How could you do this? My own fucking cousin," Vanessa started to sob heavily.

The police were outside of the door. They yelled through the megaphone, "This is the APD. You have approximately two minutes to drop your weapon and lay flat down on your face. If you do not surrender, we will take action."

"Come on Vanessa, this is not a game anymore. They will shoot you. Put the gun down!" Brandon said, begging for her to surrender.

"Tracy, you are my cousin. How could you? We were like sisters back in the day. How could you sleep with my husband?"

"Brandon, I thought you told her. You didn't tell her about us?" Tracy questioned.

"Tracy, do not listen to her. She is a monster right now. I did tell her baby," Brandon said turning around, looking at her.

"Us? A monster? You are fucking right! Look at what you turned me into. You better tell me what the fuck this bitch is talking about," Vanessa said ready to shoot. "He didn't tell me shit Tracy. If he did, why the fuck would I be doing this? He lied to you boo," she smirked. "So Brandon, basically what you are saying? You guys are together and this is your family? You just started another fucking life in Dallas."

"Yes, we are bitch," Tracy said wanting to attack Vanessa.

"How the fuck could you do this to me?"

"These may not be his kids, but he has one in the oven," Tracy rubbed her stomach.

"I fucking loved you Brandon," Vanessa said with more tears coming down her face.

"Vanessa..."

"Shut up!"

"You have 30 seconds!" the sheriff yelled.

"Miss Vanessa, this is not a game. They will take action. Please, drop the weapon," the bailiff said moving towards Vanessa slowly.

"How could you Brandon? You got my cousin pregnant. How could you? I know I couldn't have your baby, but how could you?"

"Vanessa."

"Tell me you love me Brandon."

"What?"

"Tell me you love me and I will surrender. Tell me, you do not want that baby."

"Brandon, you better not say it," Tracy said looking at Brandon as he turned around.

"She is going to pull that trigger if I don't Tracy."

"No, she isn't and you better not fall for this bullshit either. Vanessa has no heart. I am carrying your baby, Brandon. You better not because she will not shoot," Tracy demanded.

"When a black woman is angry, she will do anything at any time, bitch. You keep trying me. I am going to fucking shoot your ass before I go to jail," Vanessa said, shaking and gripping the gun harder. "I just pulled your weave out bitch. Tell me now, Brandon," Vanessa said pointing the gun at Brandon.

"I have to do it Tracy. I love you Vanessa and I do not want this baby."

"Brandon, you're a fucking ass," Tracy said in disbelief.

"Lies," Vanessa pulled the trigger.

"Down everyone!" the bailiff screamed while dropping to the floor.

Everyone dropped to the ground. The gun jammed. The policemen barged in and Vanessa released the gun and fell to the floor. They rushed and handcuffed her, and began to read her rights. The police made Brandon and his family exit the court room. Vanessa looked up, watching them leaving.

"Brandon, I fucked Darren!" she yelled. They lifted her up to exit her out of the building. She walked quickly out of the courtroom to the hallways.

"What the fuck you said?"

"I fucked Darren, you piece of shit. I fucked him at his place, our house and in our bed."

"Bitch, you fucked my ex-husband? You are nothing, but a fucking hoe," Tracy said making sure her kids felt safe.

"So, you fucked him huh?" Brandon asked while walking on the side of the police with Vanessa.

"Sir, please back up," the black officer said.

"How could you? Answer that Vanessa, you fucking bitch," Brandon said wanting to punch her.

"Sir, back up now. That is no way to talk to a woman," the black police officer stopped him.

"You know what the funny thing is Brandon," she said turning her head to the side and laughing, "I am having his baby too. Come to find out, I can have babies. You fucked my man and I fucked your man," Vanessa said, exiting the door laughing.

Brandon stood there breathing hard and angry.

Tracy walled over with her kids, "You love her, don't you?"

"I had to say what I had to, to protect my child."

"Your child? A few minutes ago it was your kids and now, it is your child. My kids and I come as a package. There is not one child. You have children, please remember that."

"Tracy, I really do not want to hear this right now. I am pissed off. Go ahead and tend to your kids. Breka is crying for you."

"I swear to God, Brandon, you better not love her or we are going to have problems. I will deal with your black ass later."

The white tall police officer came over, "We have to go down to the precinct to file a report. Please, follow me."

"This is not over, Brandon," Tracy said grabbing her kids and walking off. She stared Brandon down like she wanted to kill him.

Brandon blew with his head down following. "No, it's just getting started," he said to himself.

Chapter Twelve

Taste me and Tell Me

Old blood stains and dirty spots covered the beige wall in the jail cell. A steel bunk bed with hard cots with a light scratchy blanket lay on the top bunk beds. A steel toilet seat, a roll of toilet tissue and a white sink filled with hairs completed the room. The channel changing on the 10 inch TV made Chelsea squirm in her sleep. Chelsea dreamed about how her life played out since meeting Brandon. The sequences of lies; Brandon telling her that he loved her, them making love in her home, her stalking that didn't get her anywhere. For days, Chelsea couldn't get out of her mind how a man could lie and play with a woman. She became upset in her sleep when she heard the television.

Chelsea finally woke up from a nap.

"Cash, hey baby, what's on TV today?" she asked while rubbing her feet together with her white socks on.

"Pretty much the same thing they are showing right now, *Good Times*," Cash replied with a soft voice. Her beautiful light skin had a glow because she was in love with Chelsea.

Cash and Chelsea wore orange jail suits lying next to each other on the same cot. Cash turned towards her to give her a kiss on the cheek. She smiled, showcasing her pretty white teeth. Chelsea got a little closer, facing Cash.

"You know I love you right?" Chelsea asked, glaring intensely into Cash's pretty brown eyes.

"I know that and I love you too. You're not about to break up with me, are you?" Cash asked while sucking on her teeth. She always did this when she was worried.

Chelsea didn't say anything. She wanted to make sure that what she told Cash was the right answer.

She shook her head. "No, baby…never. I love you too much to break up with you. You have done so much for me while I have been in here. You know tomorrow, I will be going to a half-house. The fact that you are not going to be there is going to hurt me. I am going to miss you baby, so we need this time together."

"I know and I hate it. I am going to miss you so much. You know you are my babe. I love you so much," Cash kissed Chelsea on her thick pink lips.

"You know, I will not be there for a long time. You will be done here the same time I will be done there, and then we will be together. We will have our freedom. You are the first person I ever loved. I mean, I know you are aware of my situation with Brandon, but that was lust. It wasn't love. I know what love is now and I love you, Cash. You have accepted me for me, gotten to know me at face value. I really do appreciate that."

132

Tears rolled down Cash's face. "Baby, I love you too. There is so much I want to know about you, Chelsea. You are my woman. When I get out of here, I am going to make sure you are taken care of. I appreciate the fact that you are okay with my situation concerning my ex. You have to understand I wouldn't do that to you. I was out of my mind and I was hurt. Chelsea baby, I love you too much, and I know you wouldn't cheat on me. I can feel your love. You have the best love, baby. I love you," Cash said sitting up on her elbow.

"Cash, look, I understand what you did and you had to do what you had to do. I mean, I went after Brandon's wife," Chelsea said smirking. "Yo, I tried to kill that bitch with an oxygen mask. She was like, *get off of me*. She was really scared of what I was doing to her, but I wasn't going to kill her.

I wanted the bitch to stop breathing a little bit, while I was making my point. She needed to leave my nigga alone. I mean, you know when you put your heart on the line and a man plays with it, a bitch will go crazy. How can you cheat on a woman that loves you? A woman that makes you happy, but you don't want to leave your wife. A woman that can't birth your kids. Karma is going to be a bitch to her, just watch! All I wanted was love, but I have that now."

"Yes, you do," Cash started to blush.

"I don't know why they have me in here. I just wanted her to leave my man alone."

They both laughed. "You are a fool. I understand baby," Cash said, pulling a long piece of hair away from Chelsea's face. "You were in lust, like you said. I mean trust me, good dick will do that to a bitch. I know you are talking about love, but when a real nigga dick you down and suck the soul out of your pussy, it will make you do crazy shit. I mean, look at my crazy ass. I threw hot grits on my ex and cut the bitch he was in bed with, four times. These niggas think we are playing about being in love, but you know, after all that shit. You know what?"

"What?"

"It was meant for us to meet. This is what God wanted. When you walked in this cell, I saw the fear in your eyes," she started to laugh. "It was something about you, I knew you were going to be my woman. I never thought about being gay, until you ate the hell out of my pussy on that first day. You better make sure that pussy is tight when I get out, so I can fuck you. I am going to get the longest dildo, strap that shit on and fuck you like crazy," she smacked Chelsea's ass.

"Oooo, I love when you smack me on the ass. Cash, I love when you talk like that. I never ate a woman's pussy before. I didn't start liking women, until I got here. Like I told you, I was so scared of being in here that I wanted to eat your pussy, so you wouldn't beat my ass," Chelsea kissed her. "Cash, I need you to do something for me."

"Anything baby, I will do anything for you," Cash smiled. "You must want me to taste you? You know I am going to be doing that all day until you leave."

"Hell yes, but that is not it," Chelsea took a deep breath.

"What is it, babe?"

"I need to get some type of payback from Brandon. I can't sleep well because of what this nigga did to me."

"Why are you still worried about this nigga? I thought you loved me and said fuck him? I am not understanding, so please help me," Cash said backing up, looking at Chelsea with confusion.

"Baby, I do love you, but he hasn't paid for what he has done to me. I want him to pay. I want him to suffer. I didn't get to do what you did to your ex. You went after the bitch he was fucking and I did, but I didn't do anything to him. I want his marriage and everything about his career to fail."

"I am loving the way you are thinking, but tell me. Are you sure you do not love him? It has been months since you have seen him."

"I am very sure. For what he did to me and getting me banned from any flight attendant job, he needs to be fucked up. If I have to suffer, then he has to suffer as well. Maybe the dreams and anger will go away. Until then, I have to do something, so I can feel better."

"If it is going to help you, then I will do anything for you, baby. All you have to do is tell me and I will handle this nigga for you."

"For such a pretty bitch, you are a bad ass," Chelsea said spanking Cash's ass.

"I am from New York. We are loyal to everything we do and I want to show you how much I am loyal to you. I might be light skinned, but I will fuck you up!"

"I really do appreciate it, baby."

"Now, tell me the plan," Cash got out of bed and got on the floor. "I want a massage. You know I love when you massage my shoulders and do my ponytail."

"You are such a baby," Chelsea said, getting to the edge of the bed and placing her hands on Cash's shoulders.

Cash took both of her sleeves out of her suit and moved it down to her stomach. Her perky plump twenty-five year old breasts were juicy. Chelsea admired her Cherokee skin.

"Cash, I know you are going to curse me out when I tell you this, but I need you to seduce and fuck Brandon. I want you to make him fall in love with you," Chelsea said squinting her eyes and face.

Cash turned around quickly with anger, "You want me to do what? You have to be fucking kidding me, right now?"

"Cash, just hear my plan out."

"I don't want to hear no more of this bullshit. I love you and all, but what the fuck do I look like fucking a nigga you loved?"

"Cash, I told you about your temper. All we are doing is talking. You haven't even let me finished talking to you."

"Cash turned back around, waiting for Chelsea's hands on her shoulder, "Go ahead and tell me. I am sorry baby. I am working on myself."

"It's okay. Like I was saying, I need you to fuck Brandon. You are pretty and young, with a tight pussy. This would give you the chance of a lifetime to ruin a nigga's life, the legal way."

"I understand that and everything, but shouldn't we forget about this nigga and move on together? You are asking a lot. You want me to fuck him and make him fall in love with me. I don't know Chelsea."

"Like I told you, he did some fucked up shit to me and I want him to pay. Cash, I could take us around the world, if it wasn't for him. He fucked up a great opportunity for us."

"But think about this Chelsea, if it wasn't for him, we wouldn't have met."

"True, but we could have gone out of the country. I could have shown you the world, Cash. God would have made another way for us to meet. I mean, we met in jail, and I am your cell mate. I mean how is that shit going to look when we tell people. This fuckin' bastard needs to pay, Cash," she said, rubbing Cash's shoulder with force.

"I love when you get mad, but you are massaging a little too hard. I can't wait for you to eat my pussy because I think you still love this nigga."

"I swear I do not love him and I am waiting on it too, but first....listen to the rest of my plan baby. When I get to the halfway house, I am going to be good, at first. I am going to act noticeably scared and let everyone know, I shouldn't be there. After the time gets close for me to get out, I'm going to act a little crazy. I'm going to write him threatening letters and call him as well."

"You are going to get a longer sentence if you do that. You will be right back here."

"Hear me out, Cash."

"But, don't they check what you write?"

"I am going to get in good with my nurse. You know, act nice and show her that I am not crazy. Let her know I did it for love."

"I understand, go ahead. I am trying to put it all together."

"I will tell him everything that I want to do to him and then, I will write a letter where I can get caught. It should give me maybe a month or two more in the half-way house, not in jail."

Chelsea, but...."

"Listen Cash, by this time, you would have been able to seduce him and find out everything that is going on with him. I want you to fuck him so good and make him fall in love with you, that he leaves his wife and gets it all."

"I thought you said she was entitled to nothing."

"She isn't unless she has the proof that you are messing with him. He told me that when I was sucking his dick. She has to have some type of physical evidence of him and a woman together. She can say, I saw him and these messages are proof. She can use anything but text messages. You do that and everything is gone from him. After we go for lunch, I will tell you the rest of the plan."

"I love your idea baby, but he is in Dallas. How in the hell am I going to get there? I used all my funds for my lawyer."

"Don't worry about that. I got a girl out here in DeKalb named Star. She is staying at my place now in Houston. Star has access to all my accounts. She will transfer money to your account for you. I have 2.3 million dollars stashed in a secret account. I will transfer you ten grand. It will take care of food, hotel, attire and etc."

"Damn baby, why didn't you tell me about this before?"

"Cash, I had to make sure you love me and that I can trust you."

"I remember Star. Why the fuck do you have another bitch at your place?"

"Cash, I didn't know I was going to be with you. I can't ask her to leave. She is my best friend, ever since I met her in Atlanta. She has been down for me ever since I been here. She has taken care of my home and bills. She is an amazon and if you want baby, you can fuck her. She told me while I was in here that she goes both ways and she likes me. I am not going to do anything with her because I can't go from bitch to bitch, but you can. You just make sure you are tight for me."

"I told you I am…."

"When you see Star, you're going to want her. But, let's focus on Brandon. He works for the Dallas Cowboys. We need to throw him off of his game. I want him late for work. I want him to give his full attention to you, to the point that he is fired. If that doesn't work, we are going to have to go to plan b."

"And that is?"

"We're going to say he abused and raped you. Once he has too much going on in his life, they will not want him. I have been here for so long and he is out there. He is enjoying life and freedom. He is out there loving her, so he has to pay for everything he took from me," Chelsea said, staring off thinking about how she was loyal to Brandon.

"If this is what you want, I will do it for you. I am going to stay at your place with Star, right? I am pretty sure my apartment is gone."

"Yes baby, you can stay there. I have two cars as well. Star got my car out of impound, so you can have one. I know you are going to do an awesome job baby. I just need you to watch your attitude with him. No matter how much this man treats you like you are the only one, trust me, he is lying. It will be all fake knowing that you are doing this for me. His body, deep waves, lips, dark skin, bald head and muscles will drive you crazy. I mean the nigga is fine as hell, but Cash, look at me."

Cash turned around and looked at Chelsea, "This nigga will make you feel like the world is yours. He will give you the best sex ever. He will make you feel nuts and orgasms you never had before, but remember who you are with."

"You baby, I love you. I won't let this nigga fuck my head up. I want to make you happy, Chelsea."

"I am happy, baby. I will be happier when he is sad. Now, give me a kiss," Chelsea reached down kissing Cash.

"Do you want me to eat your pussy now?" Cash asked rubbing on Chelsea's leg.

Chelsea stood up, taking her hair out of the ponytail. She took her jumpsuit and let it fall to the floor. Cash looked at her, gazing at her amazing body. While in jail, Chelsea's ass and thighs got thicker.

"That nigga fucked up. You are a bad bitch!" Cash said crawling to kiss Chelsea's thighs.

"How do I taste, Cash?" Chelsea asked, gripping her tits.

"Your body taste amazing," Cash grabbed Chelsea's leg and placed it on the bed, opening them up. She stared at her pretty pussy. Cash licked her lips and stood up on her knees. She placed her pink thick lips on Chelsea's pussy lips. Chelsea moaned and Cash did too. Cash licked her lips slowly spreading her pussy lips apart with her mouth. Cash was licking her clit with no hands. Chelsea was thrilled with the tongue of Cash. It was her spot. Chelsea gripped the top of Cash's head. She stopped Cash and leaned her hand back.

"Do you love me Cash?" Chelsea asked with her mouth opened wide.

"I do baby," Cash said with juices all over her lips.

Chelsea reached down, wiped her juices off of Cash's lips and tasted herself off her fingers.

"You are going to make me a happy woman, right?"

"I will do whatever to make sure you are happy."

"Good job baby," Chelsea forced Cash's head back to eating her pussy.

"Good Cash," Chelsea smiled psychotically. "We will be together forever," she said, thinking about her master plan.

Chapter Thirteen
Darren's Love

A year before

****

Vanessa pulled into Darren's driveway. She took a deep breath looking into pocketbook mirror. Her left hand started to sweat. She was dazzling in her blue and silver t-shirt, blue jeans that showed her curves and black flip flops. She swallowed really hard. She stepped out of her black BMV convertible. Vanessa placed her black Gucci shades on with the sun beaming down her face. The cool air hit her face as fall was approaching. She walked up the cement steps and rang the doorbell.

"Hey, come on in," Darren said bringing Vanessa inside of his house. "You said you wanted to speak to me. What's up?" Darren said standing in a white t-shirt, showing his chest and grey sweat pants that showed the print of his ten inch dick. His chocolate skin, bald head and hazel eyes made Vanessa go crazy inside. She looked up to his 5'11 and fit body. She wanted to grab his shaved beard and ride his face. Vanessa was wet and ready for Darren, but she had something to let him know.

"The reason why I am coming here is because I can't do this anymore. I can't keep doing this with you. It is not right Darren," Vanessa said shaking her head. She took her shades off, placing them in her hands.

143

"What why? I mean what we have is very special, Vanessa. You can't take that away from me."

"I know it is, but I just don't feel right cheating on my husband anymore. I love him and the fact he goes to work every morning and works really hard, while I am having sex with you, is uncalled for."

"So, you are saying your profession isn't anything?"

"No Darren, I am not saying that," she blew. "I am basically saying I can't see you anymore. We can't keep having sex. You are the deacon of the church, and I work on the usher board. This is not right Darren. It's too much sin going on."

"Sin? You weren't worried about sin when I had you in the preacher's room."

"And that was wrong. I was weak at the time, Darren. I asked God to forgive me."

Darren walked up to Vanessa as she pressed against the door. She almost melted.

"I know what this is really about. This is about losing the baby, isn't it? You are afraid if he finds out that you lost our baby, you won't get a damn dime from him. Isn't this what it is about? I told you I would take care of you."

"Don't bring that shit up," Vanessa started to turn a little red, getting mad.

"Shut up. I mean, what, do you not believe me? I mean Vanessa; I left my wife and kids for you to build something with you and you want to leave me. We were in church when you said you wanted to be with me. You said you loved me. You told me that," Darren raised his voice.

She backed away from him walking slowly towards the living room. "Darren, I don't love you like I love my husband. I love him and I have to be careful, Darren. This isn't right. It's a sin and I'm feeling very uncomfortable about everything. I have a burden on my soul."

Darren looked at Vanessa. He knew she wanted him bad, so he picked her up. Vanessa gave in.

"We need to make sure we fix that right now. You do not love him. You love me. I don't know what he has done to you, but I am the man you are going to love," Darren kissed underneath her neck.

"Darren, no, we can't keep doing this," Vanessa said lightly feeling his soft lips.

He turned them around to walk to the bedroom.

"I don't want to hear another word about him. I don't want to hear anything about how much you love him," Darren walked down the long hallway to the bedroom and threw Vanessa onto the king size bed.

"You only answer to me, do you hear me?"

Vanessa was turned on, but scared at the same time. In the past, Darren was very abusive to Tracy.

Every time Tracy would go out of the house, Darren would follow her. He thought she was sleeping with the one of the deacons in the church. Many times he punched her in the arms, chest and face until he felt better about the situation. Darren took his shirt off. His chocolate abs poked out of his stomach. Vanessa was hot.

"Say his name again and watch what happens to you," Darren said dropping his sweat pants down to his ankles.

"Darren....no....I can't. Please don't do this to me."

"No Vanessa, I am going to fuck you with my big dick, so you can remember who your man is. You must be fucking him? Are you fucking your husband?" he shouted.

"No, I am not. We haven't had sex and I don't know why."

"What the fuck you mean, you don't why? I told you I don't want you fucking him at all. You are going to make me fuck you up."

"Because if he doesn't want me, he has to be cheating."

"You know what? Who cares because if he is, then we got him. It will make it easier for us to be together. I don't know why you keep dragging me along and not break up with this fool. I can take care of you and me, so drop his ass."

146

"I can't just do that, Darren," Vanessa was fearful of her life, but knew she had to give her pussy up.

"Get on your knees with your ass in the air, come to me and suck my dick," Daren said jacking his dick to nine inches.

Vanessa took her flip flops and shirt off. With no panties on, she crawled over. She licked her lips to make sure they were nice and wet for Darren to enter.

"Your hands behind your back."

I don't know if I can do that."

"Hands behind your back, Vanessa."

Vanessa placed her hands behind her back with her mouth open. Darren slid his hard dick in her mouth. He tasted so good to her. She let him keep going until she gagged.

"Say his name again and I will fuck you up," Darren looked at her as she struggled.

Vanessa dreaded to hear those words come out of his mouth. She knew Darren's crazy side was coming out. He continued to fuck Vanessa's mouth until her eyes watered. She was wet and ready to be fucked, but literally in fear.

"I won't say it again baby. I promise," she said catching her breath.

"Who said take my dick out of your mouth? Turn the fuck around and give me that fat ass you have," Darren commanded Vanessa, as she turned around and arched her back perfectly for Darren. He slid his long thick chocolate dick inside of her. Vanessa grabbed the comforter taking all of him. In and out, real slow, Darren stroked. Vanessa loved Darren's dick. He started to fuck her hard and grabbed Vanessa's shoulders to get deep inside of her pussy. She moaned loudly.

"You have some good ass pussy. You are about to make me cum, already. Shit, I can't keep it in any longer," Darren came right on her ass. He stammered taking deep breaths. "Come here and suck the rest of this nut out my dick."

Vanessa's pussy tightened up from Darren's dick. She got up, jacked his dick and swallowed his cum.

"Fuck, that pussy better had been tight. Now, take my dick out of your mouth."

Vanessa took his dick and looked at him with cum running down her mouth. She didn't know what to expect next. She had a million thoughts running through her mind. She hoped Darren wasn't going to hit her. Darren pushed her on the bed. She was lying on her back and he got on the bed as well.

"Listen, I love you and don't want to hurt you. You know I have been watching you for years, ever since I was married to Tracy. I was thinking to myself, why didn't I meet you first? Why weren't you the mother of my kids? To have an affair with you is driving me crazy. I have to watch you from the pulpit.

Not seeing you every day is killing me. I will not hurt you, like I hurt Tracy. I had reasons, but you will not give me any, because I know you love me, right?"

"Yes, I do Darren and you have to understand….."

"Good girl, now, I do understand. I know you are trying to pick the right time to leave him. I want you to understand that I need you more. I want you to come over more. I want us to go out to dinner and other things as well. On Wednesday, we shouldn't go to Bible study. I want you to come here. I am going to have dinner, wine, candles lit and music, with your favorite songs playing. I want you to understand how much I love you, Vanessa."

"Oh Darren, I never had that before," she hugged him.

"Yeah baby, he doesn't give a damn about you. I am the one God has for you."

"And I feel it. Are you sure you are not going to hurt me?"

Darren got a little closer to her. "Listen to me. I am not going to hurt you. I love you too much. The only hurt there will be is when you leave him. He is going to make the worst mistake of his life when you two divorce. You are going to be my woman," he said, grabbing her right hand and kissing it.

"Okay, baby, well I have to get ready for work in about an hour. I hope I will be able to function," she laughed sitting up.

"Vanessa, I love you."

Vanessa stared at Darren, "I love you too."

Vanessa was torn between two men and didn't know which man was right for her. She had been through it all with Brandon, but Darren turned her on and fucked her good. He also scared her. She had to think about it before Darren lost his patience.

Chapter Fourteen
Why Did You Do It

Vanessa was cuffed and rushed into the interrogation room. The short, husky, white detective with blonde hair was pissed off. The officer sat Vanessa in the metal chair and un-cuffed her. She placed her hands down the cold steel white top table, grabbing her wrists. She was crying and her heart raced. She knew she made a mistake because of her jealousy and love for Brandon. Vanessa knew she was going to prison and didn't know if she was going to survive. She swallowed with fear as the officer walked out of the room. A chandelier dangled from the ceiling with a dim light. The room felt like a scene out of a movie with the shadow grey walls. The detective walked back and forth with hot coffee in his hand. He looked into Vanessa's eyes.

"Mrs. Williams, I am Detective David Adams," he drank his coffee. "Do you know why you walked through those doors cuffed?

Vanessa brought both her hands to her face, crying her soul out.

"For the love of God, I do not want to hear it. Do you know why you are here, Mrs. Williams?"

"Yes!"

"Why are you here?"

She took her hands from her face, "I attacked my husband's mistress."

"I don't give a flying piece of shit about them. You made the swat team come into the courtroom. You better be fucking glad you dropped your gun because they were going to shoot your ass. You took a gun and was about to shoot someone."

"I was not going to shoot her or anyone in that room."

"You took a fuckin' gun from a bailiff, Mrs. Williams. You took it in anger and if my team wasn't there, you may have pulled the trigger. You know how to use a gun. Your husband said you have shot one plenty of times."

"He told you that. Did he write a statement against me?"

"Mrs. Williams, you are worried about a man and I am about to tell you the fucking charges that you are about to fucking face. You brought out my team for some dumb shit that could have been handled elsewhere. I mean, you were already up there to testify against another mistress and you pull this. I don't give a fuck about them. All I want to know is why did you do it? I mean, why did you take the gun? If you tell me the truth, that you were going to shoot her or him, it might take some years off of your charges."

"How is that going to drop some of my charges? You know what; I am not going to say another word. I want my lawyer. I know what you are trying to do."

A black woman detective walked inside of the room. She wore a black women's suit with a blue dress shirt. Her short Toni Braxton haircut was cute to Vanessa.

"You think this is a television show? You think you are going to lawyer up and everything is going to go away. No, this is real life Mrs. Williams."

"David, please. I will handle it okay," the woman detective looked at Detective Adams with discomfort.

"You are going to pay for what you did," he walked out of the room, slamming the door behind him.

She smiled lightly, "I am sorry about that. He....uhm....he just found out that his wife wants a divorce and she is leaving him for the captain."

"I still didn't deserve that," Vanessa wiped tears from her eyes. .

"I know you didn't. Hi, I am Detective Kerry Coleman," She introduced herself while sitting across from Vanessa.

Vanessa shook her hand. She started to look through Vanessa's file and took a deep breath.

"Vanessa, I am going to be real with you. I mean, woman to woman, sister to sister. What you did was wrong. I know you want your lawyer, but I really want to break this down to you. The judicial system doesn't play. You taking a gun and pointing it at people, having the swat team take action is a lot of charges. They said that your husband showed up with his mistress and kids and you flipped out. I am going to be real. I would have done the same thing, if you were telling me the man I gave everything to, played me like this. He went out and had a whole new family behind my back with your cousin. No one wants to be loyal and you damn sure can't trust your own family. I am sorry to hear and witness this."

Vanessa dropped her head down, "I gave him everything and he just goes out and makes a baby. I tried to give him babies but I couldn't. We tried over and over. He said it was okay and we would try again, but this bitch goes out and makes a baby with my cousin."

"Honey, do not beat yourself up. Please, not over a man that didn't respect nor love you. It is not worth the stress, maybe temporary, but after this, you move on. You are very pretty and have a good head on your shoulders. Don't let a man drag you down to hell. You have a great job and this is going to hurt you so much. I mean, just like the woman that tried to choke you. She lost her job for this man and you are going to as well. He keeps everything he has while you women suffer. It isn't fair to you."

"He already dragged me to hell when we were married. I am here. I am going to jail or prison for this."

"Vanessa, if you keep calm and show everyone you did it as an act of love, you can do a lot of probation and community service. You were just on the stand about to testify against one mistress. You can beat this."

"Why are you helping me?"

"I know what you are going through. I really do. I watched my mother go through it with men in her life, until she was killed right in front of my eyes."

"I am sorry about what happened."

"It's okay. She met a man that was very abusive and controlling and one day she didn't listen to him. He was drunk. He walked in when I was lying next to her, moved me out of the way, and shot her five times. I was five years old when I witnessed that," Detective Coleman stared off into space. "I know what you are going through. I want to help women like you. You do not deserve this. You deserve real love from a man. When you get free, you need to move on from him.

Vanessa, get a divorce and leave him. You need to leave all the memories from him and start over, a new beginning. You guys have been together, but what you are going through, is a slap in the face."

"Detective Coleman, thank you so much. I really do appreciate it. You have no idea"

"You are welcome. You are going to have to go to a holding cell for today. You will see a judge tomorrow, so get on the phone with your lawyer and get yourself out of here."

"Thank you so much," Vanessa stood up as Detective Coleman came around for a hug.

"It is going to be alright. Go ahead and give it to God. Let go of the devil in disguise. He is not good for you."

"Thank you. Can I tell you something else?"

"Sure, what is it?" Detective Coleman sat on the edge of the table.

Vanessa sat back down and rubbed her stomach. Detective Coleman smiled with excitement.

"Congrats girl. Do you know what you are having?"

"No, not yet. The doctor called me the other day."

"So wait, you are saying, Mr. Williams got you pregnant?"

"Here is the thing. I am two weeks pregnant. I do not know if it is my husband's baby or my secret boyfriend, Darren."

"Vanessa……"

"Darren is Tracy's ex-husband."

Detective Coleman mouth dropped and Detective Adams walked into the room.

"We have to wrap this up and send her to the cell. We just got two more cases," he said closing the door.

"Vanessa, you have to follow me. We will talk about it later. You make sure to get on the phone with your lawyer. Everything will be just fine."

They walked out of the room to the holding cell. Vanessa was scared. She went and sat down on the hard bench. Two other inmates were in there, but they looked scared as well. Vanessa had twelve hours to think, make a call and get herself out of this situation. She just closed her eyes and began praying to the Lord. Hopefully, a blessing was coming.

"Mrs. Williams, I want to really hear what were you thinking about when you took my bailiff's gun yesterday? Please, approach the bench, come into the center and tell me, " Judge Rock said sitting up, taking off his glasses.

Vanessa looked at her lawyer and stood up in fear. Tears started to roll down her face. She started to approach the bench and saw Darren walk into the room. She smiled. She walked to the center and looked at the judge.

"I am waiting, Mrs. Williams," he said very impatiently.

"Your honor, I have gone through a lot in my life with my husband. I am broken and hurt. First, we couldn't have a baby. Next, I am getting attacked on the plane by one of his mistresses with an oxygen mask. Then, I see another mistress that he has gotten pregnant. I am human, your honor. My temper was in a rage, but I was not going to shoot. I just wasn't thinking. I mean, I am mad. I am an angry black woman. This man has hurt me so much. I have shed so much tears that I have none left. To see that yesterday, hurt me. I don't know what you are going to sentence me with, but I am not a monster. I just found out the other day that I am pregnant by that man back there. He is going to be a great dad. He is a deacon and I know I am going to be happy with him. I am going to let my husband move on and do his thing. I am going to let him sign those papers. I don't even want whatever it says on there. He can have it all. I just want a new beginning. I want to be happy with the man God has for me, right behind me. I am sorry for scaring you yesterday. I am sorry for everything that happened," Vanessa closed her eyes and opened them, hoping the judge didn't sentence her to months and years in jail.

"Mrs. Williams, you pointed a gun at people, even putting kids in danger."

Vanessa knew right then, it was over. The lawyer hung his head down and Darren looked in fear.

"I am so sorry, your honor," Vanessa begged and cried.

"I am talking."

"I am so sorry, your honor. Please forgive me."

"I am talking Mrs. Williams, but yes, you are human. I understand what you did and this is your first offense. Here is what I am going to do. I am going to give you five years of probation and 100 hours of community service. Are you okay with that?"

Vanessa soul jumped for joy, "Yes, I am, your honor."

"Go back to your seat and stand."

Vanessa walked back over smiling at Darren.

"Mrs. Williams, I am giving you five years of probation and 100 hours of community service. This court room is adjourned."

Vanessa hugged her lawyer with joy. She skipped to Darren and gave him a hug.

"I love you baby," Darren said kissing her and grabbing her ass.

"I love you too."

"Are you really pregnant?"

Vanessa was scared to tell him the truth, "Yes, yes I am."

"Why didn't you tell me?"

"I was going to tell you Darren, but I didn't know how. I didn't want you to be upset with me."

"Baby, I told you, that was the old me. You showed me how to be a better man. I am not going to hurt you. I told you that."

The lawyer walked over and hugged Vanessa.

"Oh, great speech Vanessa," Duncan, the lawyer, said smiling at Vanessa.

"Didn't you see me talking to my woman man?" Darren said looking eye to eye with the lawyer.

"It's okay Darren," Vanessa said looking shocked.

"I am sorry about that. I will fax and call you tomorrow," he said walking over.

"Thanks. Darren, what was that for?"

"Did you fuck him too?"

"Why are you acting this way for? You know I haven't. You are the only person I am messing with."

"I am just being careful."

"Darren, I love you and only you. Baby, we are about to have a baby."

"You are damn right," Darren smiled. He hugged her tighter. Vanessa was happy and hoped the abusive love was going to come to an end. She was praying Darren's heart had changed.

Chapter Fifteen

Brandon Meets Katrina

2nd Base Bar and Grill in Dallas, Texas was crowded. Cowboys' fans surrounded the place with Aikman's, Emmitt's, and Irvin's jerseys. Special team coach and Brandon sat at the bar low key drinking beers and drinks back to back. They were celebrating Thursday night's victory.

"You son of bitch, you did it!" Coach Carter said taking a shot of gin. "I mean a 4-4-3 defense on the one. I mean Brandon, gutsy call. Bring it in and give me a hug," he gave Brandon a light hug.

"Come on man," Brandon laughed. "You can't do this before you have us on TMZ sports."

"I'm sorry. I love you buddy."

"I love you too man."

"We might be 5-3, but I think the cowboys can go all the way this year. I mean, Romo is looking great out there man. The defense is energetic. The whole organization and the fans are behind us. I mean, look at this shit Brandon. Fuck, I love it."

"I think so too. The energy and love I have received has been outstanding."

"I am glad you are here man. This is your year."

161

"It really is. I have a great job. I have a new start in life and I feel good. Bartender, give me and Coach Carter another round."

The bartender nodded and began fixing their drinks.

Coach Carter twirled in his seat looking at the crowd. "You know what man? It's a Friday night. My wife is overseas for the weekend, my kids are at their aunt's house and I am drunk with a stiffy."

Brandon laughed, "A stiffy? What the hell is that man?"

"I am fucking hard, Brandon. Come on, you piece of shit. Look at the nice pieces of ass in here. Check out the blonde with the big tits. Isn't she gorgeous?"

"Kyle, you are a married man. You know your wife would kill you, if you cheated. She might be overseas, but you are well known in this city. You know she will find out."

"Let me tell you something, Brandon. I have cheated on Kathy plenty of times. We are coaches for the Cowboys. All we do is win and fuck," he said laughing. "This isn't college or high school man. Some of us have yacht parties with a bunch of chicks and fuck them in the middle of the sea. Everyone is doing it. It is too much pussy out here, Brandon. I love blondes and big tits."

"How can you guys be so discreet, being one of the biggest team in America?" Brandon asked getting drinks from the bartender.

"Let me give you some knowledge brother. We have discreet forms. They are forms, where the only way we can fuck, is if you sign. It also discloses that you can't tell anyone that we fuck. Damn Brandon, what the fuck did they do at Georgia Tech?"

"I heard something like that, but I was married man. All I was worried about was getting here. It has been my dream to be a Cowboy."

"Look Brandon, your engaged, I get it. She is 6 months pregnant. Her tummy is sticking out and she is having mood swings and tempers all the time. The sex is going to stop and look nasty with a pregnant woman. I have plenty of forms man. It's going to be one chick that will show up and blow your mind. Do you want them?"

Brandon started to think, "Yeah…..I just want to look at them. I love Tracy man and I have been doing great with her. I don't think I am going to cheat on her, but anything can happen, if she would leave me."

"That's my guy. I will get you those forms on Monday, but I am about to go over here and introduce myself to this blonde and her friends. Are you coming?"

Brandon looked behind and shook his head no.

"Alright man, I am going to get me some victory pussy. I will be back," Coach Carter walked over grabbing a beer.

Brandon looked up at the TV from the Cowboys highlights. He started to think about everything that transpired in his life with Chelsea and his ex-wife. He was still angry that Darren and Vanessa were together and she was 4 months pregnant. He wanted to pick up his phone and text her, but he didn't. He saw his phone lit up and it was a text from Tracy. She sent him a photo of her and her two kids, sleeping on her stomach. He smiled and text "awww." Brandon was happy with Tracy, but the fact that her kids' father was the man his ex-wife was with, disturbed him. He placed his phone back down and took a shot of gin.

"Bartender, another round and a pitcher of beer, man."

"Bartender, I would like a Hennessey and coke, thank you," a soft voice spoke.

Brandon turned to the side and spotted a gorgeous light skin woman, sitting next to him. She wore a tight black Gucci dress that showed her curves. She crossed her legs wearing no panties. Brandon saw the panther on her right leg. He looked her up and down, smelling her perfume that blew him away. She looked at him and smiled. Brandon started to smile and was nervous. He wanted to look back, but he thought about Tracy and his future baby. Did Coach Carter jinx process already?

"Here you two go. Coach Williams, here is your gin and pitcher and miss, here is your drink," the bartender said coming over. "Your drink will be...."

"Brian, you can put it on my tab," Brandon said grabbing his drinks.

The bartender nodded.

"Brandon, is it?" she asked, licking her lips with thick lip gloss. "That will not be necessary. I will pay for my own drinks," she said handing him a $20 bill out of her Gucci pocketbook.

The bartender walked off.

"I'm sorry if I offended you miss," Brandon looked at the woman.

She looked at him with her long hair, pulling it to the right, "it's okay. I don't like men buying me drinks. I work too. You might think I owe you something for a $10 drink."

"Not at all. I didn't catch your name."

"My name is goodbye," she stood up and walked off. Her black heels clicked as she switched her slim body and fat ass.

Brandon gazed at her, as she left her scent. He never got a type of response from a woman like that before. He turned back to watch the game, but was confused.

"Bro, I seen that big piece of ass come over here. Did you get those numbers?" Coach Carter walked over, holding onto Brandon's shoulder.

"No, she wouldn't let me buy her drink. She walked off with an attitude. I hate black women like that."

"She doesn't know who you are. She thinks you're a regular guy. Go over there and let that piece of ass know who you work for and who you are, Brandon. These women are nothing, but a nut until we go home to our women."

"I have to know her name. I will be right back," Brandon said getting out of his seat.

"Just, no fucking, until you get those forms."

Brandon walked over where the woman was standing, by the jukebox.

"Hey," Brandon stated nervously.

She turned around, "Hey. Are you stalking me or something, because I didn't let you buy me a drink?"

"No, I just wanted to apologize, that is all. I am sorry about that."

"It's okay. I guess it's a guy thing to buy a woman a drink. I shouldn't have thought you were like every other guy that does it, trying to get me in bed."

Brandon smiled, "I forgive you. What is your name?"

"My name is Katrina and you are?"

"My name is Brandon. I am the defensive coordinator for the Cowboys."

"Oh wow, it is nice to meet you Coach," she said drinking, while looking at Brandon's bulge in his brown dress pants.

Brandon noticed it, "You ok there?"

"I am. I am just checking you out. I guess this is the part where I am supposed to give you some pussy, because you're a coach."

"No, not at all. I am just making conversation. I mean, you are very gorgeous."

"Thank you so much. What are you doing here, Brandon? You are very tall, nice teeth, dark skin and after what I just saw, seems like you have a big dick."

Brandon laughed, "I am for real. I just wanted to chat with you, Katrina."

"Sure Brandon, I am just going to keep it real with you. I am from New York, that's what we do."

"Oh yeah, what part?"

"The Bronx."

"Okay cool. Well to answer your question, I am out celebrating yesterday's victory."

"Well congrats. Have you gotten some congrats pussy yet?"

"You are very blunt, aren't you?" Brandon started to think should he say he was engaged. "I haven't. I have a baby on the way."

She was puzzled and didn't know what to say.

"Well, congrats again. So, you and your wife are expecting? That is great."

"Well, yeah….we are."

"What Brandon? What were you going to say?"

"We just got divorce, but we're still going to have the baby. It was just too much turmoil."

"I am sorry to hear that."

"I have messed up in the past and I can accept it. I lost a good one over a woman," Brandon stated.

"How did you lose her?"

"I cheated on her. The woman I cheated on her with is in jail for trying to kill my wife."

"Wow Brandon, that sounds like a book. You have so much drama in your life," exclaimed Katrina.

"I did Katrina. That was in Atlanta, but I am blessed to be here in Dallas and be a Dallas Cowboy. Everything is going well and I couldn't be happier."

"Your ex-wife, is she here in Dallas or Atlanta?"

"She is in Atlanta. She is married to the deacon of the church I used to attend."

"I am sorry to hear that, you poor man."

Brandon got a little emotional, "I was a fool Katrina, and none of those women deserved it. I shouldn't be here. I shouldn't be having this great job, but God forgave me. I am so thankful. I am sorry. It might be the beer and shots making me feel like this."

"It is okay. I am just shocked that you have been very honest with me. What is your curfew?"

He smiled, "I am grown."

"You might be grown, but you are the coach for the Cowboys. You know guys can't be out late. I am surprised you are out this time of night."

"It is 9'oclock."

"I am going to be real with you Brandon. I am new to the city. I am at the Hilton about ten minutes away. I haven't fucked in a long time and I need to be fucked. I have magnums there. I want you to fuck me, if you think you are up for the challenge."

Brandon wanted her bad, but knew he had to go home to Tracy.

"Are you really thinking if you want to fuck me or not? You must think, I am going to tell someone? I just want some dick, that's it. I don't care if you are a coach."

"No...I was just picturing you riding me, that's all."

She placed her drink on the jukebox, "I am in suite 246. Leave about 10 minutes after me. I want to take a shower."

"Don't I need your number?" Brandon asked hoping it wasn't a set up.

"No….just open the door and let the fun begin," she said smiling and walked off.

Brandon and other men looked at her as she was exiting the building. Coach Carter walked over, "You are going to need a form with that piece of ass."

"I am going to need a vasectomy. I swear, I am going to take that condom off and cum in her."

"Brandon, she might look nice, but that bitch might be the devil in a dress."

"I am going to take my chances. Do you have any forms with you?"

"I have one, just for me."

"Let me get it man."

"Brandon, come on. I got a piece of ass that wants to go to a room."

"I need her man. I am the new guy, please man," Brandon said begging for a form.

"Okay," They walked over back to their seats to get the form from Coach Carter's jacket.

Brandon hugged him, took another shot of gin and walked out, calling Tracy. He explained that he was too drunk to drive home and he was going to spend the night over Coach Carter's house. She was okay with it. Brandon got in his car and headed to see Katrina.

Chapter Sixteen

Pussy Too Good....Fuck It

Brandon got into his truck and sat there. He wanted to make sure everything in the form was correct. He wanted things to work out with him and Tracy, but they haven't had sex in three weeks. Brandon was horny and ready to bust a nut. He started up his truck, pulled out of the parking lot and drove off. He picked up his phone and called Vanessa. The phone rung four times before she picked up.

"Hello," Vanessa answered the phone.

Brandon was shocked she picked up, "Hello Vanessa, how are you?"

"Brandon, what do you want? It is late."

"I am just calling to check on you."

"You sound drunk. You don't need to be checking on me. You need to be checking on your new wife to be."

"I am just seeing how your pregnancy is going. That is all."

"Brandon, I really don't want to talk about it right now."

"I know you are mad at me, but I want to hear how do you feel about being pregnant? I mean, finally you are pregnant. How does it feel?"

There was complete silence over the phone.

"Brandon, I am not pregnant anymore. I lost the baby the other day," she started to sob.

"I am sorry. What happen? Why didn't you tell me?"

"Why Brandon? You fuckin' hurt me. If you didn't care about what you did to me, why the hell would I tell you about being pregnant with another man's baby? Oh now why, because Vanessa can't keep or make a baby!" she shouted.

"Vanessa, I know I hurt you and I am so sorry, but I still care for you. We were together for a long time."

"Listen Darren, just walked in. I have to go," she hung up really fast.

"Vanessa?" Brandon was kind of worried about Vanessa. He pulled into the Hilton and parked. He stumbled out of the truck and walked into the building.

The front desk male clerk noticed who he was and said, "Go Cowboys."

Brandon fake smiled and walked to the elevator. He pressed up and walked in. He chose 2 and pressed his body against the door. He had the form in his back pocket. He looked in the elevator mirror noticing his white sport polo shirt was crooked. He fixed himself as the door open. He walked out and went to the right to the rooms. He slowly walked to door 246, second guessing if he should do it. He was at the door and placed his hand on the knob.

He opened the door and walked in the gorgeous suite. The view from the Cowboy's stadium was amazing. He walked in further seeing Katrina coming out of the curtains. She was naked. Her flat stomach and tats turned Brandon on. Brandon dick grew instantly in his pants.

"I was about to start playing with myself. I thought you weren't going to show," she said walking towards Brandon.

"No…I just had to get myself together, that is all," Brandon said, giving her a kiss as she placed her lips on his.

She grabbed his hands and walked towards the view. He watched her fat ass switched. He was ready to get out of his clothes. Brandon turned to the right of him and saw them in the mirror. He was mesmerized by her. She grabbed his shirt and started to take it off. She began to lick on his dark nipples. She made her way to his chest and abs. She kissed slowly and caressed his big dick outside of his pants. Her tongue made her way back to his neck and started to suck on it.

"Wait….before we do this, I need you to sign something."

"What is it?" she asked very horny.

"It is a form pretty much saying when we have sex, that you can't tell anyone."

She smiled, "Really? Well, I don't have a pen on me. Do you?"

Brandon forgot a pen, "I don't either."

"We can get one later," she said, unbuckling his pants. She pulled his pants and boxers down at the same time.

She got down on her knees and started to suck his dick. Her mouth felt amazing with no hands. Brandon looked into the mirror watching her head bob back and forth on his dick. She spit on his balls and massaged them at the same time.

"You have some big balls. You have a lot of cum in them. I am ready to drain them dry," she said putting his dick back in her mouth.

Brandon was happy. His phone started to ring. He was scared of who it was.

"You need to get that?"

"Yeah…I don't know who it is," Brandon said bending down grabbing the phone out of his pants pocket. Katrina continued to suck his dick. When he got his phone, it was Tracy. He didn't know what to do.

"Sit down right here on the couch and answer it."

Brandon sat down, hoping she wouldn't say a word. He answered it and she continued to suck his dick.

"Hello," he said about to moan.

"Brandon, did you guys make it there safe?" Tracy asked half-sleep.

"Yeah, we are just getting here."

"Okay, I was just checking on you baby. I love you. I will see you tomorrow."

Brandon hesitated, "I love you too."

"Okay, good night," Tracy said hanging up.

Brandon hung up with Tracy while looking at Katrina sucking his dick.

Brandon was hoping she wouldn't stop, "I am sorry about that."

"There is nothing to be sorry about. It is time to fuck me now, nigga," she said, stroking his long dick shooting straight up. "Sit back and let's get the rest of these clothes off of you," she said while pulling his pants, shoes and socks off. She reached for the condom beside her and placed it on him.

"Damn, you have a big ass dick. My ex was like six inches. I hope I can take it."

He grabbed her, getting her on top of him, "Let's see."

She grabbed his dick and she was very tight. She wrapped one arm around his neck as he sucked her tits. She finally let him slide it all the way in. Both felt amazing to each other. The cold weather painted the sex.

"Your dick feels so fucking good. Oh my God....shit...Brandon," she said going up and down on him. "I can feel it in my stomach," she looked into his eyes and started to kiss him. She couldn't resist the great feeling from him.

"Does that dick feel good to you?" Brandon asked looking into her eyes, grabbing her ass to go deeper.

"Yes daddy....Oooo...fuck me...fuckin' fuck this tight pussy nigga."

"What's my name?"

"It's Brandon."

Brandon was loving her tight pussy. She was the best pussy he ever had.

He thought Chelsea had the best, but Katrina beat her by a long shot. He picked her up and started to fuck her in the air. He looked to the left, so she can see herself being fucked.

"You see me fucking your pussy."

"Yes I do," she said grabbing his neck, so she wouldn't fall.

"Do you see that shit?"

"Yes daddy, I see it."

He placed her down on the couch on her back and slid in her. He felt so amazing to her. She started to kiss on his neck and scratching his back.

"This is some pussy, you marry…fuck…you have the best pussy ever," he said stroking, making her feel every inch of him.

"Do you want to take that condom off, so I can feel you?"

"Hell yes," Brandon slid out. He took the condom off and slid right back in her.

They didn't care what they were doing because the sex was amazing. Brandon looked into her eyes and started to kiss her with passion. He kissed on her neck. She grabbed his ass to get deeper until he touched her g-spot. He was long to do it but too thick to get to it. She started to squirt and squirm, but Brandon kept fucking her. Her breaths and moans were out of control. He never had anyone ever squirt before and knew he had her right where he wanted her. He stopped stroking as her mouth was wide open.

"Are you okay?" he asked sliding out, seeing his dick wet and the couch as well.

"Oh my God," she moaned with her legs shaking. "I never squirted in my life. It's like, I'm still squirting."

"How does it feel?"

"Oh, fuck you," she said leaning up to suck his dick.

He placed his hand on top of her head. Brandon felt his nut getting closer and closer when she stroked his dick with her hand.

"You are going to make me nut if you keep doing that," Brandon said with his toes curling.

She stroked faster and sucked the tip of his head. Brandon felt a rush.

"Katrina, I got to cum."

"Right in my mouth baby."

Brandon grabbed his dick and nut right in her mouth. His cum dripped down her chin and she scooped it in her mouth before it fell on her leg. She looked into his eyes and he looked down feeling joy. She moved his dick and jacked it until all of his nut was out.

"Oh my God, that was so good," his body shook.

She stood up walking slowly to the bathroom. Brandon sat down on the couch smiling.

"Are you okay?"

"I am...I have to walk it off. You fucked the shit out of me."

"That pussy was good."

Katrina walked to the bathroom to brush her teeth and pee. Brandon grabbed his phone to make sure that he didn't answer a phone call. He looked and saw a text from Vanessa.

The text read, *Brandon, I miss us. I want you back. I lost my baby because it should have been from the man I loved and married. Don't text back because Darren is here. Please, let me know baby. I will talk to you later.*

Brandon sat back on the sofa very confused about what was going on. Katrina walked out of the bathroom.

"I am going to need for you to leave now," Katrina said, fixing her hair.

Brandon was shocked by what she said. He couldn't go home, especially after he just fucked her. "Are you serious? I am drunk."

"Brandon…I said, come fuck me. I didn't say anything about you spending the night. You fucked me very good and now, I just want to crash."

"Okay," he started to get all of his stuff together to put on. "Are you going to sign the form? I see a pen by the TV."

Katrina laid in the bed naked, "No, I am not going to tell anyone. I am too tired to sign it."

"You told me you would sign it," he said zipping his pants up.

"I know, but maybe, another time."

"Katrina, I really need you to sign it."

"I am not a fucking groupie. I am kicking you out. All I wanted was some dick and that is it. Now, it is time for you to go."

Brandon put his shirt over his head. He was very nervous.

"Are you sure you are not going to tell anyone about this?"

"I promise I won't," Katrina said getting under the covers, turning the television on.

Brandon started to walk towards the door.

"It was nice to meet you and fuck you."

"You too, I hope you have a great season, Brandon."

"Thank you," he said opening the door and looking at her. "Hope to see you soon."

"You will…."

Brandon closed the door and started to walk down the hall. He didn't know what to expect. He called Coach Carter, hoping he didn't have a woman at his place.

Katrina reached over to get her phone. She made a call.

"Hey Star. What's up? Have you talked to Chelsea?"

"Yeah…she called today wondering did you find him yet?"

"I sure did. I fucked one of the players last week and got information about where he was going to be."

"Great job….did you fuck him yet?"

"I just did. You have to tell Chelsea, I can't follow through with this plan. I feel bad doing this to her. I love her and I just can't."

"You know, she is not going to like this at all."

"Star, I know….but fuck…..like she said, that nigga is too good. His dick is too good."

"Trust me I know. I fucked him, but hang in there. Chelsea gets out in four more months."

"I can't wait to see her. Also, let her know he is about to have a baby as well. She didn't tell me anything about this or maybe, she didn't know."

"Damn…ok. I will, hey, I got to go. I have company. You hang in there and keep fucking that nigga until he is weak."

"Okay, I will," Katrina hung up the phone. She knew if she would keep going, she would fall for him. She was already having a moment when he made her squirt. She was going to try her best to keep her word.

Chapter Seventeen

Chelsea is Out

Chelsea sat down on the edge of the bed. She was excited, but mad as hell. It was her last day at the halfway house. Chelsea was upset because Brandon had a baby by another woman. Brandon also told Cash that he loved her. Cash kept her word that she would keep seeing Brandon. He flew them both to Vegas the month before the baby was born. He even got her into the skybox for the playoffs, where the Cowboys lost in the first round. She was thinking that could have been her having his kid. That could have been her skybox.

Chelsea wanted Cash to make him fall in love, not get free treatments and trips. She was highly upset and couldn't wait to be released. Footsteps got closer to her door and she lifted her head up. She was dressed in flight attendant clothes, the last attire she wore, the day she almost killed Vanessa.

The knob turned and it was Nurse Tasha. She came in walking slowly with a smile on her face.

"Baby girl, you did it. You are finally free," Nurse Tasha said. Chelsea came towards her with a smile on her face and hugged her.

"Thank you so much, Ms. Tasha. You have been a big blessing. You have been so great to me. Thank you."

"Baby, you just make sure you don't do anything stupid like that again. Do you hear me?"

"Yes, Ms. Tasha."

"Okay….let me walk you out," Nurse Tasha said, walking towards the exit door.

Nurse Tasha and Chelsea walked out. Chelsea looked down the hallway. She saw the door with sun shining through the facility. Many nurses and patients waved goodbye.

"Chelsea, you have my number. If there is anything I can do, please let me know," Nurse Tasha said hugging her.

"You know I will and I will be coming to your church, as well."

Nurse Tasha opened the door and Chelsea exited, feeling the cold air hit her face. She walked outside and down the steps. She saw her lawyer, Rebecca, parked outside in a heavy red jacket standing next to her Honda Accord. She rushed to her and hugged her, as Chelsea came down her last step.

"You did it," Rebecca smiled.

"You did it. Thank you so much for everything and the advice you gave me."

"No problem at all. Chelsea, make sure you do not do anything dumb like this again. Please get yourself together. Make sure you get Christ in your life. Do not let another man mess your life up. Please Chelsea."

"I promise you. I am better than that. You know, being in jail and here opened up my eyes. Rebecca, thank you."

A blue Ford Mustang pulled up beside Rebecca's car. It was Star in the car.

"Chelsea, we got to go now ma," Star said rolling down the tinted window.

"Chelsea, do not do anything stupid. I am serious. You might not get any slack this time," Rebecca said hoping she heard her.

"I got to go Rebecca. Thank you again," she hugged her again then quickly walked to the car.

She opened the door and the car aroma was filled with weed.

"Bitch, you finally got out!" Star said smiling.

"Girl yes, it is time to fuck this nigga up. You made it sound like something is wrong. Is something wrong?"

"Girl, I have to give you the scoop on all of this shit that is going down, for real. Cash and I have been putting in work for you. I fucked niggas that I wouldn't think about fucking, but you gave me a car and roof over my head. That is loyalty right there."

"Girl no problem, but please, tell me what the fuck is going on? Now, this baby, did you guys find out who the bitch is?"

"Yes, the bitch Brandon has a baby by, is the bitch Vanessa's cousin. Check this, Vanessa is engaged to her ex-husband. His name is Darren. I mean the shit is fucking crazy and she lost the baby. I mean this shit is straight out of a book, for real."

"How did you find out all of this?"

"Brandon can't keep his mouth closed soon as he gets some good pussy. That is how we got the scoop on Vanessa, but I fucked Brandon so call best friend, Coach Ricky Carter. He has been telling me everything."

"He works with Brandon?"

"Yes honey, some white guy. He is very sexy, but has a small dick. Anyway, I fucked his ass to the ground and he gave me the scoop on everyone. He stays drunk after work and he will tell it all. I guess he figured, I wouldn't tell anyone. The child is now one month old. They are out of the playoffs. Cash is at the crib in Houston. She and Brandon just got back from DR for the weekend."

"This bitch is going everywhere with this nigga."

"Chelsea, you told this bitch to make him fall in love with her. He is fuckin' in love with her. She is fucking him good. He is giving her cash and that's great because she doesn't have to spend your money. She has been loyal and done everything you told her. Now, look bitch, you can't get mad at this bitch for doing something you wanted her to do. She is still your woman. She didn't want to do the shit in the first place. You just make sure she still loves you and

Brandon hasn't fucked her brains out. You know that nigga got some good long dick."

"Hey!" Chelsea shouted.

Star laughed, "Bitch, is you mad?"

Chelsea fixed her face, "I don't know what I am because that should have been me. Why the fuck is she getting all of this shit done?"

"Chelsea, he fucked you good and you went fucking crazy as hell. That's why. Now look, the plane leaves in two hours. I have to turn the car in and we will go home and get this shit together. I am tired of fucking this nigga. He gave me an agreement form where I had to shut my mouth, so whatever you do Chelsea, do not say a damn word. I can get sued. Okay?"

"I got you. I think it is time to switch the plan up. I will find out everything. If this bitch is too happy, it is time to pull the trigger. This bitch can't get all of this and I am not getting a damn thing."

"You still love Brandon, don't you?"

Chelsea didn't say anything.

"If you do, get your nigga. He should be happy to see you."

"Not after the fake letters I sent him and that one phone call. He wouldn't want me."

"Chelsea, you never know baby."

"Yeah…"Chelsea looked out the window, hoping Brandon would forgive her and want her back. She didn't know how to pop back into his life.

The baby was hollering in his crib. Tracy walked into the bedroom and picked up little Kayla. She walked over trying to calm her baby down. She sat on the edge of the bed and saw Brandon phone lit up from an incoming call. She looked at it and it was Tommy.

"Brandon! Brandon!" Tracy yelled, "Someone name Tommy is calling you. Who is my princess? You are, yes you are."

Brandon rushed in.

"Who is Tommy?" Tracy wanted answers.

"One of the new trainers we are getting on our team. It might be important and my phone has to charge. Can I have a moment to myself?"

"Let's let daddy handle his business," Tracy gave Brandon a kiss. He kissed his baby as well. She closed the door.

They walked out and he picked up on the final ring.

"Katrina, you almost got me caught. Didn't I tell you, I would call you?" Brandon whispered.

"Baby, I know, but I missed you and I needed to hear your voice."

"Katrina, we just got back from DR yesterday. It hasn't even been 24 hours yet. I told you I would call when I am not around my child and fiancé."

"I know Brandon, but I love you. This isn't right anymore. You said you would leave her."

"I will, but she just had my baby. I have to leave at the right time. I don't want her to put me on child support."

"So, pretty much what you are saying is that you are not going to leave her because of a baby? I mean, she is fucking ugly as shit. Brandon, I am the bitch you want to be with!" Katrina yelled.

"Wow….I never heard you talk like this. We just got back from vacation and you are acting crazy. You need to calm down. I told you, I will call you when I get some free time. Where the fuck are you anyway? I mean, where are you staying now, since you never want me to pick you up from your location."

"I am staying with a cousin until I get on my feet. I told you that, Brandon. I told you she doesn't want people to know where she lives."

"Okay Katrina, listen I have to go in here, so I will call you when I get some time. It might be today or tomorrow, but it will be sometime this week," Brandon heard Tracy coming back.

"That is bullshit Brandon and you know it."

"Whatever, she is coming, so I will talk to you later," Brandon hung up the phone.

Katrina threw her phone down on the ground. She had a glass of wine in her hand. She lounged around in orange boy shorts and let her breasts hang. Her phone rung and it was Chelsea.

"Baby, you are out!" Cash yelled in excitement.

"Yes, I am…How are you doing?"

"I am doing good baby. I am ready to see you."

"I can't wait to see you as well. How's everything with the plan?"

"The plan is doing great. He is in love with me."

"Okay great, Star and I are turning the car in now and going to catch the flight in an hour. I will see you at 1pm. You know how to get to the airport, right?"

"Yes baby, I will be there to pick you ladies up."

"Okay Cash, I will see you later on today."

"Okay baby."

Cash hung the phone up. She was torn between the two. She loved Chelsea, but she wanted Brandon. She never had a man take her anywhere and be a gentleman to her. She never took a big dick and had plenty of orgasms. She didn't know what to do. Chelsea's voice played in her head when she warned her about Brandon. "This nigga will make you feel like the world is yours. He will give you the best sex ever. He will make you feel nuts and orgasms you never had before, but remember who you are with." She didn't want to go through with the plan because she didn't want to mess up her chances with Brandon.

Chelsea hung the phone. Star walked over to her.

"What she said? Is she going to be able to pick us up?" Star said holding her Coach bag.

"Yeah....she has fell for Brandon."

"How do you know?"

"I can hear it in her voice. Let's get back to Houston, so I can get my man."

Star and Chelsea started to walk toward the shuttle to head to the airport. Chelsea knew she had to have plan B, just in case Cash did fall for Brandon.

Chapter Eighteen

He Loves Me.....The Fuck?

Chelsea and Star walked out of the Houston airport. They looked to the right and saw Cash. Cash got out of the car and walked fast pulling her jeans up and being careful in her 6 inch heels.

"Oh baby, I am so glad you are home. I miss you so much," Cash said kissing and holding Chelsea.

"I miss you too. I love you so much," Chelsea said kissing her again.

They walked to the car, put their luggage in and drove off.

Chelsea sat in the front seat with Cash as they held hands. Star was in the back seat on her phone.

"So baby, how are you doing?" Chelsea asked, letting go of Cash's hand.

"Everything has been going good. I am following the plan, but overall, I missed you. I love you so much Chelsea. I mean, you have no idea how much I do. I am so glad you are home."

"Me too baby....How is Brandon looking?" Chelsea wanted to see something.

"He is looking the same, since when you last saw him."

"Come on Cash. Is he working out? Did his dick get bigger? Is he trying any new tricks? I mean, tell me something Cash."

"Okay….baby…he has been working out more. He has an eight pack now. If you were to see him now, you wouldn't think he was a coach. He is built like a football player."

"Really, and the dick?"

"Come on baby, don't ask me that."

"Cash, it is okay, I know he has some good dick. We all have fucked him. Did he get bigger?"

Cash paused hating Chelsea reminded her that they fucked Brandon.

"Cash….Can you hear me? Did he get bigger, babe?"

"His sex is very good. He gave me plenty of orgasms and he has grown an inch."

"Oh, is that right? Are you sprung over him?"

"Chelsea, baby, I love you."

"I understand that Cash, but are you falling for Brandon?"

Star lifted her head up waiting to hear Cash's answer.

"No, I am not. I have had better dick before."

"Okay, you never had an orgasm before, but you have had better dick than Brandon. Okay sure," Chelsea said getting mad on the inside.

"Why are you acting like that?"

"Because you can be straight up with me Cash. If you are falling for him, let me know. You are not even the same girl when we were locked up. You're not even saying bitch this or bitch that. You are talking like a woman who has been treated right and with class. Where the fuck is the bitch I was locked up with?"

"First of all, I am a woman with class, you should know that. Chelsea, that was jail talk. Before we met, I was a manager at Stone's grocery store. I was a loving girlfriend. I have always had class. You only knew what I wanted you to know, until we got the fuck out," Cash pulled in Chelsea's driveway and got out.

Chelsea got out as well. "I told you Cash, not to fall for him. I told you that he would make you feel like you mean the world to him. I fucking told you he would fuck your brains out, because that is how he gets you. You didn't listen to me."

"Are you jealous because he is taking me to dinners and out of the country? This was your fucking plan," Cash walked off heading into the house.

Chelsea walked behind her fast, "Bitch, am I what?"

Cash turned around. "Are you jealous? You are mad because I am getting all of these treatments and you didn't get anything. You told me to do this shit, Chelsea! You did. I didn't want to do this shit in the first fucking place. You knew the nigga was fine and could fuck. Why the fuck did you do this to me? I was always in love with you, we had something special Chelsea."

"What are you saying, he is about to break us up?"

"Chelsea. I am not saying that. I didn't want to do it," she started to shed tears.

"I mean, what do you want me to do, huh? What is the plan Chelsea? Am I supposed to call rape on him now? Am I supposed to get him fired? Tell me what the fuck you want me to do, so I can be over with this shit. This is fuckin' crazy.

We are doing all of this shit for a fucking man. Let's just move forward and be with each other. You got me and Star fucking niggas for you, like we're your fucking hoes. I don't like this shit at all."

The room was quiet.

"I love it. I'm getting tickets to the games and getting cash on the side. I am going to milk my cow as long as I can," Star said looking at Cash.

"I really do think you are in love with Brandon, Cash. It's time to pull the plug on this plan, asap, so we can be together."

"Sure, we can do that, because you run every fucking thing. You never ask me, am I happy?"

"Happy with what?"

"You didn't ask me, am I happy with him?"

"Bitch, you better not be happy with him, Cash."

"I am Chelsea. He makes me feel like a queen."

"He did that to me Cash. He did the same shit he did to me that he is doing to you. You are just fuckin' sprung off his dick."

"Chelsea, he makes me feel like the world is mine," Cash started to shed more tears.

"Cash, you need to get this over with now. You are in too deep."

"Y'all, Coach Carter told me that Brandon is going to be at Roses' restaurant at 8pm and he wants me to meet him there as well," Star said, reading her text message.

"Where is that?" Cash asked waiting for a response.

"He didn't text me an address yet."

Chelsea started to think, "He took me there. It is a restaurant here in Houston."

"Are you sure?" Cash asked getting a glass of water.

"She is right. He just text me the directions," Star said looking at Chelsea.

"Why the fuck is he coming here? We just went to DR this weekend. How can he get away from her and the baby again?"

"Maybe he's bringing her here or recruiting," Star said looking back in her phone.

"This nigga is recruiting another bitch," Chelsea stared off in space.

"No....no....Chelsea, don't say that at all. He is supposed to love me," Cash slams the glass on the counter.

"You think so huh? If you do not get a text about it, then you know, it is another piece of ass."

"He loves me Chelsea; he is going to call me to meet him there."

"You are so fucking stupid. He thinks you are in Dallas. He doesn't know where the fuck you stay, Cash. This is another woman, watch," Chelsea said walking down the hallway. "I am going to show you. Ladies, let's prepare for the grand finale tonight. We are going to fuck his life up tonight," Chelsea said her voice fading as she headed to her room.

A couple of hours went by. The ladies dressed up. Star wore a silver mini skirt, black shoes and hoop earrings. Chelsea wore a navy skirt that hugged every inch of her body, lip gloss that thickens her lips and 6 inch black heels. Cash wore black flats, light blue jeans and a black t-shirt, with her hair in a ponytail.

"Okay Star, you have to go ahead and leave. It is already 7:30p.m. The place is 15 minutes away. I will text you to find out where you guys are sitting. Please, let me know how he reacts when he sees you. He is going to shit on himself."

"Hell yeah, girl. Okay, I will see you later," Star said walking out of the door.

"Okay Cash, as you can, tell he didn't text nor call you. You saw with your own eyes that he and Carter are going to be at the restaurant. I am going to show you that he doesn't love you. After this, we will go back and be with each other. I am the only person who loves you baby. You know that," Chelsea said, fixing her dress in the mirror in the hallway.

"Chelsea, I can't believe I felt he did this to me. I should have never done this."

"It's okay, because you did it for me. I told you, when I found out where they are, I am going to send you the picture of her."

"Let's go, so we can get there on time," Chelsea said walking to the door.

Cash and Chelsea walked outside the door, got in the car and drove to the restaurant. At 7:52p.m., Star text that she was with Coach Carter and Brandon wasn't there yet, but he was on the way. Halfway there, Star confirmed that Brandon was there with a woman that was light skin. She said he was nervous and looked away from Star. Chelsea told Cash and she started to cry.

"Are you okay?" Chelsea said parking the car in the restaurant parking lot.

"No….I am a fuckin fool Chelsea," she placed her head on the window.

"Girl, dick will make you do that. I am about to get out and go in. I will text you, so be ready for anything. I'm going to spoil his surprise. I'm going to scare this nigga and then, you can pop in and let everyone know that you are fucking him and he raped you. You didn't sign that paper, right?"

"No, I didn't. I wasn't going to go with this plan, but now knowing he has another bitch in there, I'm going to fuck his life up."

"That's my girl. I will text you when to come in," Chelsea got out of the car fixing her dress. She walked slowly. Star told her that they were just a few tables from the bar. Chelsea couldn't wait to see the look on his face. She walked in and heard jazz music playing. She was greeted by a hostess, but she let her know she was going to sit at the bar. Chelsea walked over to the bar looking for Star and Brandon.

She sat down, looked over to the right and saw them. She saw Brandon, but couldn't see who he was with because Star's thick body was blocking the girl. She ordered a drink, looked over again and still couldn't see her. Chelsea stood up and looked over. When Star laughed, her body shifted. She looked at the woman and saw Vanessa laughing, as well. Chelsea's heart dropped. She sat back down in shock. Her heart started to race.

Her plan wasn't for Cash to come in. Her plan was for Brandon to lose his date, come to her and hopefully, fuck her. She took a sip and paid the bartender. She stood up making noises with the bar chairs. She looked over to him. Brandon heard the noise and looked over to see her.

"Shit," Brandon said hiding his face.

Vanessa asked, "What is wrong Brandon?"

"Chelsea is out."

"Huh?"

"Look Vanessa, Chelsea is out."

Vanessa looked up. "That is impossible. She has a lot of time to do. Oh my God. This bitch is out."

Star and Coach Carter turned around.

"It's okay, I have a restraining order on her," Vanessa said looking at her.

Chelsea walked off and left the restaurant. She was furious. She walked back to the car.

"Baby, what is wrong?" Cash asked wondering why she was upset.

"Cash, let's go right now."

"What? What about the plan? Who is he with, Chelsea?"

"Cash, you are not going to like it."

"Tell me Chelsea. Who is he with?" Cash asked about to cry.

"Cash, he is with his Vanessa, his ex-wife."

Cash sat back in her seat shocked.

"Let's go. Fuck the plan. This nigga...I just can't keep doing this shit. If I get closer to her, I can get locked up. It is not even worth it. I am sorry that I put you through this. Let's just go home, move on and focus on our relationship. I can't do this. I have only been out for a few hours. Let's go home."

"I am not going any fucking where. I want the nigga to come out, so I can see him and his bitch."

"Cash, it is not worth it. Please, let's go home."

You got the keys to your other car right? The one Star drove."

"Yes."

"Take it. I will bring Star back home. I have to have closure first."

"Cash....."

"Chelsea!" Cash shouted. "Please, let me handle this."

"You better not do anything dumb," Chelsea opened the door and got out.

Chelsea slammed the door and Cash wiped her eyes. She reached underneath her seat. She got her pocketbook and pulled out a handgun pistol.

"You think you can fuck all these bitches and get away with it. If anyone is going to have you, it is going to be me. I'm going to settle this shit the right way. Fuck this Brandon."

"This bitch is going to have to die," Cash said, placing the gun back in her pocketbook, waiting for them to come outside.

Chapter Nineteen
Will Marry You?

Cash sat outside waiting for Brandon and Vanessa to come out. She was furious. She couldn't believe Brandon was messing with his ex-wife. She didn't know what was going on. She heard talking approach the parking lot. She let the window drop down a bit to hear the voices. She heard laughing and Brandon's voice. She adjusted her seat back, so they wouldn't see her.

"Hey guys, it was nice meeting you, Jennifer," Brandon said fake smiling at Star. He shook her hand.

"Yes it was. We should exchange numbers, Jennifer. You know, have a little spa date." Vanessa said giving Star a hug.

"Baby, I think Jennifer has better things to do," Brandon said squinting his eyes. "Ummm, matter of fact, can I talk to her for a minute? It will only take a minute, Coach."

"Sure…I'm drunk," Coach Carter said.

Brandon walked her over to where they couldn't hear their conversation. Vanessa looked strangely at Brandon to see what was going on.

"So, your real name is Jennifer?" Brandon said quietly.

Star smiled. "You know what I smell. I smell shit. Especially, when I came in that bitch, I bet you shitted on yourself," she laughed.

"This was a setup, wasn't it?"

"Brandon, what the fuck are you talking about?"

"Chelsea, you knew she was out, didn't you? Where is she staying? Does she still have the same place?"

"For a nigga who is engaged and sneaking around with his ex-wife, you sure ask a lot of questions. Especially about a bitch that isn't his."

"This isn't a game Star. This shit is real. How the fuck do you know Coach Carter? How did you get here?"

"All I am going to say is that you better watch your back. You know karma is a bitch, Brandon. The funniest thing is you think you know your real friends and you don't. You tell all your business and think everyone is your friend."

"What the fuck are you talking about? Did someone tell you something? What do you know?"

"Jennifer, daddy is ready to go and have some of that milk chocolate baby." Coach Carter laughed. "Brandon, come on man, finish this another time. I'm horny man."

"Do you know Katrina, Star?" Brandon put one finger towards Coach Carter.

"Brandon, you heard him, wrap it up now," Vanessa raised her voice.

"You heard your wife Brandon. You better sign those consent forms," Star walked off laughing.

Brandon took a deep breath turning around watching Star walk off with Coach Carter.

"Good night Vanessa. Good night Brandon. I will see you at work man," Coach Carter wrapped his arms around Star, got in the car and drive off.

Brandon walked towards Vanessa.

"Brandon, what did you and that bitch talk about?" Vanessa asked, watching Brandon walk towards his truck. "Do you not hear me talking to you?"

Brandon unlocked the doors and jumped in the truck. Vanessa got in.

"Shit, .I am being set the fuck up. These bitches have been playing me the whole fucking time."

"What are you talking about?"

Brandon started his truck up and drove off. Cash lifted her seat up. She turned the ignition on and followed them.

"Vanessa, listen….you saw Chelsea, right?"

"Yes, when did she get out?"

"I don't know, I guess the other day."

"How did she know where we were going to be?"

Brandon didn't answer.

"Brandon answer me…How did she know?"

"You are not going to like what I am going to say to you."

"You fucked her, didn't you?" Vanessa's eyes stayed glued on Brandon.

"She, Chelsea, and I had a threesome."

Vanessa sat back in the seat. "I can't fuckin' believe this. You are a fuckin' dog. You know what, I don't even know why I am here with you. Why did my dumbass call you? Why did I let you back in my life? I am such a fuckin' fool."

"You did it because you love me. That is why, don't act like you don't know. You didn't want that baby to be his, you wanted it to be mine. I am not the only one who has been doing fucked up shit. Did you forget that you are doing the same thing as well? You have a great guy, that's what you tell me, so why the fuck are you with me? The answer is because you love me, that is why," Brandon said making a left turn into the hotel parking lot where they were staying.

"You know what, I am going home. I am done with you, Brandon. This time it is over. You go back to your sluts and leave me the fuck alone. My dumbass. These bitches might fuckin' tell Darren. I have a god man, shit…my dumbass."

Brandon parked the car and they both got out. "No one is going to tell Darren. They do not give a fuck about you! You know what? You are right. You are fucking right. I have too much shit going on, because unlike you, I have a child to take care off."

Vanessa stopped walking, feeling offended, "I can't believe you said that. You are a fuckin' ass."

"No, Vanessa, because you are worried about yourself and that's it," Brandon opened the door and walked to the elevator with Vanessa behind him.

"I'm not. I was worried about us. I tried my best to give you a baby and you say some shit like that to me. You are a fucking ass, Brandon," Vanessa said while getting on the elevator.

The elevator became silent stopping at the second floor. They got off with Vanessa wiping her tears away. They walked to the door and into the room.

Vanessa went in the bathroom to get her stuff and began packing.

"Vanessa, are you really going to go? You don't want to fuck one more time before we end all of this?" Brandon said taking his white dress shirt off.

Vanessa turned around walking out of the bathroom. "You really think I am a slut, don't you?"

"You did cheat on me, so what does that make you? You sure aren't a saint," Brandon said wanting to fuck her.

Vanessa stared to pack her suitcase. She got her clothes from the closet and put them in it.

"Fine, that is cool. I will fuck one of my new bitches, if I have to. This is why I left. You never want to fuck when I'm ready. Get the fuck out of here. I'm a mutha fucking Cowboy," Brandon said lying on the bed, watching her pack.

Vanessa didn't say a word. She finished packing and walked out. She slammed the door loudly and walked to the elevator. She pressed the ground floor button and the door opened. It was Cash. She got on and smiled.

Vanessa stood by her with her head down, wiping her tears. Cash looked at her holding her handbag tight. She had her gun. She wanted to blow her head off, but felt sorry for Vanessa.

"Men, huh?" Cash said with a smirk.

"Excuse me," Vanessa said fixing her voice.

"We only cry, at this time of night, when a man has hurt us."

She faked smile, "Yes, honey, you make sure you have a man that will be true and not lie to you. These niggas ain't shit," Vanessa said walking out of the elevator. Cash walked out behind her. She wanted to follow her but didn't. Cash walked out of the building to her car. She got in and drove off.

Cash pulled up to Chelsea's house. She got out the car and slammed the door. She walked quickly to the door and walked inside. Chelsea stood in the kitchen with a glass of Grey Goose and orange juice in her glass. She was drunk.

"Did you see that shit?" Chelsea said taking a sip, "That nigga played you."

"Bullshit...Chelsea. You fucking knew that shit was about to happen. This was all your fucking plan, wasn't it?" Cash asked clinching her handbag.

"Cash baby, what are you talking about?"

"Don't fucking baby me, bitch? I think you knew he was seeing her. You knew I was in love with this nigga and you wanted me to fuck him up if your plan didn't go through. You fucking knew this shit. You and Star played me."

Chelsea smiled, "Bitch, you are not just a pretty face huh? You see, I knew you was still in love with that nigga. You lied to me in the fucking car. You talk about loyalty and shit, but I knew that dick made you betray me. I had to show you, Cash, that you were just another nut to him."

"That is bullshit Chelsea. I am more than that to this nigga. You are mad because he took me places and bought me things. You just mad, bitch," Cash said, still clutching her handbag.

"Hoe...why would I be mad at you? You are a broke bitch. You remember who took care of you."

"I am going to fuck you up, ho," Cash said ready to fight. "Call me out my name one more time!"

"You do that and you'll have nowhere to stay. You better think twice about what you are about to do."

"Fuck you and fuck your place, bitch. Bring it, bitch!" Cash yelled getting close to the kitchen.

Chelsea took another sip of her drank, "Bitch, I'm not worried about you."

"I told you not to call me another bitch," Cash said running towards her. Chelsea threw her drink in Cash's face. She couldn't see and Chelsea threw a punch to her head. She grabbed Chelsea and threw her to the floor, while wiping her eyes. Once Cash's vision was clear, she got on top of Chelsea and started to punch her in the face. Chelsea blocked her punches.

"Bitch….bitch….bitch," Cash said spitting and punching her.

"Get off of me," Chelsea begged for Cash to get off of her.

"No, you are a fuckin' hoe," Cash stopped punching her and turned her head to the right. She threw up on the kitchen floor. She held her stomach and kept throwing up. Chelsea got up and ran to her room. Cash felt nauseous and had a strong feeling she was pregnant. She fell to the floor, grabbed her stomach and starting to cry.

Chapter Twenty

I am 100% Sure………Brandon

Cash tried to get in touch with Brandon for three days, but he didn't respond. Finally, on day four, he responded. Cash told him that she wanted to meet at *Icons* Downtown Dallas. She informed him that it was urgent. Brandon agreed and they met thirty minutes later. Cash got to the bar first and sat at the booth in the back. She bit her nails because she was nervous. She took a sip of water from her glass. Cash's handbag laid next to her. Brandon entered *Icons* angry. He looked around for Cash and walked to the booth. He angrily sat down.

"What is wrong with you, woman? Why the hell are you blowing up my phone? Tracy almost saw your number pop up on my phone. What do you want?" Brandon looked at Cash with his eyes on his phone.

"Brandon, I have something to tell you," Cash said reaching into her purse.

"So, whatever you have to tell me couldn't wait?"

"No, this can't wait any longer."

"Well, whatever you have to say, you need to hurry because I have to meet Tracy."

I don't care about where you have to be. Fuck her! When are you going to leave her, Brandon? You said that we were going to be together."

"You're crazy as hell, you know that."

Cash became upset, "Do not call me that, because I am not crazy. You told me you loved me Brandon, now I'm fucking crazy because I'm ready for you to leave her."

"Can you hurry up and tell me what you have to say? Shit!" Brandon quietly demanded.

"When I tell you this, please don't get upset or yell."

"Me...get upset about something you're about to tell me. This better be good, because trust me, whatever you have say, I couldn't give a damn about. I am a fuckin' Cowboy," he threw his hands in the air. "I don't even know why I'm here".

"Is that right?"

"Yes, that's right! Now, what do you have to say, because I am about to walk out of here if you don't hurry up."

"I don't think you are going anywhere, once I show you this."

"What you got to show me?"

She reached into her purse and grabbed the pregnancy test. She hesitated to show him and slid it on the table to him. He looked down at the test and looked up at her with shock.

"What is this?"

"You have seen that plenty of times. You know it's a pregnancy test. I'm pregnant Brandon."

He scoffs repeatedly, "Pregnant....You're pregnant....that's not mine. That is another nigga's baby."

"It's yours."

"I know what this is. You know Chelsea and Star, don't you? You were a part of their plan, wasn't you?"

"Brandon, you need to be worried….."

"I fuckin' knew...I knew I shouldn't have fucked with you. Shit."

"I know her. She was my girlfriend while we were locked up."

"Girlfriend? You bitches are on that sick shit. You set me up, but you supposed to love me."

"I do love you, Brandon. Please....I threw up coming here. Please, just let her go, so we can be together. Brandon, just leave your ex-wife and let's move. The three of us can go somewhere else."

"I am not leaving my job. Damn it, Katrina....You better listen…..and I mean you better listen to me good. We will never be together. All that stuff I said to you were lies. I just wanted to have sex with you a couple of times before I got married and that's it! I am not about to lose the love of my life for you or that damn baby your ugly ass is carrying. Do you hear me? I am getting married next month. I'm going to give you some money, so you can get rid of it. How much do you need?" Brandon asked reaching for his wallet.

Cash threw water in his face, "How dare you? How dare you talk to me like that? How dare you talk about your baby like that?"

"WHAT IS YOUR PROBLEM WOMAN???" Brandon yelled while standing up and backing into someone.

"That is right. What kind of fucking problem do we have here?"

Brandon turned around and it was Tracy......

Prologue

Part III The Birth...

"Aaahhhh...Oh my God...please get this baby out of me," Cash said, grabbing the rails on each side of the hospital bed. She laid there drenched with sweat and gasping hard in her polka dot hospital gown.

The ceiling lights beamed in her face as the nurses prepared everything for the doctor to come in. She held his hand tight, inhaling in and out deeply with her. He looked into her eyes. He wore a brown long-sleeved dress shirt with khakis. He scuffed the floor with his new pair of brown dress shoes. Doctor Bates walked in.

"You have to breathe, Katrina. You are doing a great job. I am very proud of you. I am here with you," he said, looking at Cash and wiping the sweat from her face.

"Nurse Betty, how far apart is she?" Doctor Bates went to the sink to wash his hands and scooted the small rolling chair to Cash.

"Doctor, she is fully dilated. This baby is ready to come out now."

"Okay, Ms. Young, I am going to need you to breathe. Ok? You remember your breathing techniques, right?"

Cash shook her head yes, breathing slowly.

"Okay because your little princess is ready to come out and be with her mother." Doctor Bates lifted her gown past her stomach. "Okay, she is ready. Ms. Young, 1, 2, and 3 push, okay. Can you work with me honey?"

"Come on baby. You can do this. I love you," he said, holding her hand.

"Doc, can you please hurry the fuck up?" Cash said, getting aggravated.

"You have to calm down Ms. Young. We have to make sure we are on time for the delivery. Okay, go ahead and push," he said with his hands out between her legs.

Cash breathed and pushed with force. She couldn't believe she was having his baby. She knew she was going to be happy to have him by his side. Their relationship was a secret and she finally had him. She knew he was going to be a great father to their child.

"I see the crown of her head. Come on Ms. Young, go ahead and push one more time," Doctor Bates said with excitement.

Cash gave it her all. She screamed and squeezed his hand until she felt like she almost broke his fingers.

"Yes, there she goes. It is a baby girl," Doctor Bates said, holding the baby as she cried loudly.

"It is okay. Nurse? You are about to be with your mommy. Sir, can you cut the umbilical cord?"

"Yes sir," he said, grabbing the scissors from the nurse.

Doctor Bates wrapped a small blanket around the baby and walked to Cash, handing the baby to her.

"Here is your mother. She is gorgeous, Ms. Young. You have a very gorgeous baby."

"Thank you, Doctor Bates." Cash cried as Doctor Bates handed her the baby.

"You are my baby. Oh my God, you are my baby. I am going to love you. Your father and I are going to make sure you are loved first. I love you. You are my everything." She cried with him, wiping her tears away.

"Do you have a name?"

"Yes, we do, her name is Alexus," he said, smiling at his baby.

"That is a gorgeous name. I am going to give you two a second and then we will have to make sure she is healthy." Doctor smiled and walked out of the room with the nurse.

The wooden door closed and in the small mirror was Vanessa, looking into shock. She covered her mouth as she watched Cash holding her baby, smiling with him...

Chapter Twenty-One
How Could You Brandon?

Brandon turned around and it was Tracy. Tracy gripped her brown Coach bag tighter. She was in a rage and wanted answers.

"Brandon? Oh, what are you deaf right now? What the hell is going on here?" Tracy looked at Cash with intentions to beat her ass.

"Look, I don't want any trouble." Cash stood up from the booth.

"Bitch, you better sit your dolphin face looking ass down."

Cash didn't sit down and stepped down from the booth. The customers started to focus their attention to see what was going on.

"You see; it's always bitches like you that always want to say something. Bitch, I wasn't even talking to you hoe, but you take one more step, and I am going to beat your ugly ass!" Tracy yelled, ready to fight.

Cash's face tilted. "First of all, bitch, I don't think you know who you are talking to. I will beat your ass right now and I know you are not talking, with your ugly ass raccoon face."

"Ladies, can we go somewhere and talk about this? This is not the place and my job is on the line if you act up." Brandon saw that the focus was on them.

218

"We are doing this right here. Fuck you, Brandon!" Tracy stormed at her but Brandon grabbed her.

"Tracy, I just said not here," Brandon said, trying to control Tracy.

People started to pull out their phones. The manager started to walk over. The black young, tall, slim manager came over. "Is there a problem here, Coach?" he asked, gaping at everyone.

"There is no problem at all. I have it under control." Brandon backed Tracy away from the booth.

"There is a problem. I want to get answers from this bitch. I want to know why the fuck she threw water in his face, and why is he up here with this man face bitch! Get the fuck off of me!" Tracy yelled.

"Bitch, I told you to watch who you are talking to." Cash rushed towards Brandon, trying to hit Tracy, but the manager grabbed her.

"Okay, you have got to go because people are recording you guys. Coach if these women fight, I will have to call the police and I don't want to mess up anything that you have going on."

"Let me go," Cash said, trying to get away from the manager.

"I am not going to let you go. Now, stop it," the manager said, holding her and walking towards the door.

"Bitch, come outside with your ugly ass. Fight me bitch! I am tired of all you side bitches trying to fight me about this nigga. I am the fucking bitch he wants to be with. I am pr-" Cash tried to fight the manager off of her but he took her outside.

"What the fuck was that bitch about to say? Was she about to say she is pregnant?" Tracy smacked Brandon in the face. "You better not have another woman pregnant and I just had your child! Is she pregnant?"

Brandon swallowed his pride after being slapped. "No, Tracy, sit down. Where the hell is my child? How did you know I was here?" Brandon asked, guiding her to the booth seat. "Can everyone, please, stop recording? It wasn't that big of a deal. Thank you," Brandon said, walking to his seat and looking at everyone.

"Brandon, you got a lot of nerves asking me questions right now. Do you know that? While your black ass is up here with another woman, talking about God knows what. I think the only person that should be talking is you. I want you to be real with me, Brandon and tell me why are you up here with her?"

"Tracy, come on baby," Brandon said, swallowing hard.

"Do not baby me, Brandon. Answer the fucking question right now."

"Well, can we go home and talk about it? Everyone is looking at us and I don't want to be on the news. I am one of the Dallas Cowboys' coaches. Do you know how it is going to make me look? Please, can we go?"

Tracy laughed. "Do you honestly think I give a fuck about you being with the Dallas Cowboys right now? You don't want to be on the news? You were about to be because I have my pistol in my bag. Brandon, you think you can cheat on me and get away with it. You think you can knock me up and everything is going to be fine. You think I am a fucking baby momma and I am supposed to do nothing. You really think I am Vanessa's dumbass? Is that what you think?"

"I don't think that at all." Brandon shook his head.

"I am a woman. I am a mother and I am a Queen. For you to disrespect me, not only through your fucking texts messages, phone calls, but in person too. I don't get you Brandon. Why were you meeting her up here? What did she have to tell you?"

Brandon wiped his mouth in disgust. "You looked through my phone?"

"Nigga, if your black ass don't start talking." Tracy opened her bag and reached in it. "Nigga, I am fucking crazy. I protect my territory. You better start talking right now."

"I am going to be real and I want you to calm down. Do not do anything crazy, ok?"

"I will let my pistol decide that. You just flap them thick ass lips." Tracy placed her bag down.

"Don't get crazy. It's not worth it."

"Brandon, just tell me right now."

"Okay, she is a cheerleader for the team. She got my number from one of the players because she needed to tell me something. I receive a phone call because I thought she was in trouble or something. I knew you would be mad if I met with her, so I didn't tell you about it. We met right here and she started to tell me about feelings that she had towards me, how she wanted to have my baby and marry me. I told her no because I was getting married and that is when she threw the water in my face. I mean, baby, that is it. I swear to you that is what happened. You know I love my family. I love you and I only want to be with you."

Tracy dropped her head down. She knew Brandon was lying.

"Is there anything else, Brandon?"

"No, baby. I love you," Brandon said, looking deep into Tracy's eyes.

Tracy unzipped her bag and pulled out papers and pictures. She placed them on the table. She laughed. "You know what is really funny about this shit? You are looking dead in my face declaring your love for me and my children when you know that you are lying to me."

"What are these papers that are on the table?" Brandon's heart started to race seeing himself holding hands with Cash. He knew he was busted.

"How about we look at this picture? Hmmm…this looks like the same bitch that was in here that you are holding hands with. It seems like you are in nice place out of the fuckin' country. Umm…let me guess…Dr.-"

"How did you get this picture?" Brandon asked, picking it up.

"Don't worry about how I got the picture. Now, let's look at this text messages. Hmmm…this was recent. Do you remember this text?"

Tracy showed him a text message that said that he loved Cash.

"That is not my text, Tracy."

"Brandon, is this not your fucking phone number? You need to stop playing games with me and admit that you fucked up. I am tired of you niggas fucking with my feelings. Darren left me and now, you are using me. You live in my fucking place! It is my home and those are my kids and you know what? You have to get your shit out of my home. You have until night time to get all of your shit, or I will call the cops and tell them some shit that will mess up your career. If you want to be a Cowboy, you better come get your shit from my house. Tracy stood from the booth. "Oh yeah and another thing Brandon…the wedding is off. I am done. Nigga, fuck trying to get married this year. I know you are only doing it so you won't go on child support, but you know what? Be ready for child support and seeing your child on the weekends. Oh, I forgot, you have to work. Goodbye, Brandon."

Tracy got down from the booth. She started to walk off but backed up to whisper. "I know the bitch is pregnant. I saw her glow. You are nothing but a piece of shit. Fuck you!"

Brandon couldn't say anything because he knew he was busted. He was furious. He knocked the cup off of the table and slammed his hand down on the table. The manager walked over from calming down Cash.

"Coach, is everything okay with you?" The manager asked.

"I am just a little upset, that is all. You know black women; they are always trying to start with you. I am sorry about this. It was totally uncalled for. These women were supposed to be with women with class, but as you can see, they are ratchet bitches. Be careful who you end up with. That is the best advice I can give you. I am sorry, again." Brandon held his head down in shame.

"I really appreciate that and the apology. Thank you," he said, shaking Brandon's hand.

"I will see you later." Brandon walked out of the building. He got into his truck and headed home. He called Coach Carter but he didn't pick up. He hung up and it rung. It was Cash.

He answered yelling. "What?"

"Brandon, don't what me at all. That fucking bitch is going to get it. I swear to God. How could you let her talk to me any kind of way?" Cash shouted.

"She is the mother of my child, Cash. You are a side chick that hopes to get a man soon. You don't love me. You just love my dick and the trips we went on. You are not fuckin' pregnant either. I don't know who fucking pregnancy test you have, but bitch, you are sick. My thing is, how did she find out and get pictures of us?

Did you have something to do with that? I mean, these are clear pictures of us on the beach."

"Brandon, I was with you. I am pregnant and you are the daddy. You need to accept that. Okay, I was made a fool of, thinking you and I were going to be an item and you ask me about this shit?"

"Why shouldn't I? You were in it with Chelsea before." He smiled. "You think I should trust you? You are nothing but a liar. All of you hoes are not shit."

Cash started to cry. "I love you Brandon. I might have tried to set you up before, but I love you. I fucking love you man and I am having your baby. I don't deserve this one bit. I said I was sorry and you keep holding this against me."

"Stop it, stop telling these lies. You know you are not pregnant by me. Cash, let me tell you something. You and I are over. Okay. You were nothing but a side chick and that is all you will ever be. You were a side chick to me and you were a side chick for Chelsea. That is all you will be, so whoever baby that is, good luck. You-"

"You think you will talk to me any kind of way and neglect your child? Okay, Brandon, that is all I will be is a side chick? You have not heard the last from me. You will pay for what you have done. I know how to make a man like you miserable. You better enjoy the playoffs because this is the last time you will be a Cowboy. You fuckin' asshole."

Brandon hung up. "I have to leave these black women alone. They are not good for me."

225

Cash was still parked in front of the bar. She wiped her tears and started her car up. "Brandon, you think you can just go around and hurt women and get away with it. We will see."

She pulled out and drove off. Parked across the street was Chelsea, smiling. She knew everything was headed downhill and that she could be the one Brandon would marry.

Chapter Twenty-Two

I Know You Were With Him

There was a loud knock on Vanessa's see-through office door. Vanessa was glowing. She knew she had a good man in her life and that is all she wanted. She knew he showed his true colors when he hit her, but she loved him. She knew he loved her. Her white dress shirt and her gray skirt showed her figure quite well.

"Who is it?" Vanessa smiled, looking at the roses on her desk that Darren sent her.

"Mrs. Williams, I wanted to know if I could leave early. My sister is having her baby and I don't want to miss it. Do you mind?" The white tanned blue-eyed woman asked while gazing at the roses.

"Sure. I am about to leave in a little bit myself. You have been doing a great job anyway."

"Thank you so much. P.S… you have a good man, Mrs. Williams. I mean the roses, the lunch dates, and the glow you've had for a while is ecstatic."

"Thank you, Joanne. He is a good man and I love him. I thought there weren't any good men left, but Darren has shown me there are."

"Okay, I am going to leave now. Enjoy your day," Joanne said, closing the door.

Vanessa's phone lit up and it was a text from Darren. She read it.

Baby, I am ready for you to come home. I have a surprise for you. I love you. I want to be with you for the rest of my life. I am so glad that God has blessed me with you. Come home baby. I love you. I'll see you when you get here.

Vanessa smiled and her pussy drenched her gray skirt. She logged out of her computer, got her things, and exited the door with her roses. She walked down the hospital halls with a smile and people saw how happy she was. Vanessa exited the building and walked to her car. She got in and drove to Darren's house.

When she arrived, she parked and had a flashback of Brandon. She thought about how he took advantage of her. She shook her head to get rid of the image and got her things and walked to the door. She stuck the key in and walked in the house. It was dark and there wasn't a sound. She placed her things and the roses on the stand. She walked to the kitchen.

"Darren! Darren! Baby, are you here?" Vanessa asked, looking confused.

She walked into the living room and saw Darren sitting on the couch, looking at her with a creepy smile.

"Didn't you hear me calling your name, baby?" Vanessa walked onto the carpet getting closer to Darren, who sat on the couch.

Darren paused. "I did." He stood up wearing a wife beater and black jogging pants that shown his dick print. He walked over to her. Vanessa felt the vibe that he was going to rip her clothes off and fuck her. She couldn't wait to feel his dick. Her pussy was very tight and wet, waiting for him to enter. He stood in front of her face breathing hard.

"Vanessa, you are the woman I want to be with. You are such a good woman and I will be damn if another man takes you from me."

"Baby, no one will take me away from you." She tried to touch him.

"Please, let me finish talking. I want you to fully commit to Christ and me as well. I am devoted to you and I love you."

Darren got down on one knee and Vanessa's eyes grew wide with shock. Her heart raced and she became nervous.

"Baby, I know I don't have a ring right now because I am a thousand dollars short, but I tell you what I do have and that is a heart that loves you." He held her hand. "Vanessa Denise Williams-,"

"Yes!!!" Vanessa screamed before he even finished his sentence. She tried to hug him but he stood up." "Darren, what is wrong, baby?"

Darren walked to the couch and grabbed papers. He walked back over to her and threw the papers in her face.

"So, guess what I found? Pick it up and see what I found," Darren said, breathing harder.

Vanessa knew it was her divorce papers that she didn't sign. She lied to him and told him that she signed them and that she would get her last name changed.

"Pick up the fucking papers, Vanessa, before I make you pick them up with your teeth," Darren demanded with a strong voice.

Vanessa picked up the papers hoping Darren wouldn't hit her.

"Do you know what those are?"

"Yes," Vanessa said in disbelief.

"Those are fucking divorce papers you didn't sign. You told me you signed the papers. How the fuck can I marry you and you are still married to him? Why did you lie to me? You know I do not like liars." He pointed in her face.

"Can you stop yelling at me?" She asked, flinching every time he spoke.

"Vanessa, right now, you better stop stalling or I am going to beat your ass." Darren walked up to her while looking into her eyes.

Vanessa was scared. "Okay, baby. I didn't sign them-"

"Because you are still in love with him, that is why. Huh? Is that it?"

"No, I am not. I love you, Darren."

"So, why didn't you sign these fucking papers?"

"I have been busy with work and I wanted to get more from him, baby. I was still in talks with my lawyer. I am sorry that I didn't sign them yet. Please, don't be mad at me or hit me. I love you. I promise you that you are the only one I love and want to be with, Darren."

"Do not tell me you love me and don't sit up here and fucking lie to me."

"Baby, that is the truth." Vanessa started to wipe her eyes from crying. She tried to hug Darren again. He walked off back to the couch. He grabbed a folder.

"Do you see this?" he asked, shoving it in her face. 'Do you know what is inside of here?"

"No, I don't. Baby, what is it?" Vanessa started to shed more tears.

He opened it and it was three pictures of her and Brandon from the night of the hotel. Vanessa placed her hands over her mouth.

"Darren...please, let me explain. But first, how did you get these? Oh my God, Darren, I am so sorry." Vanessa's heart dropped to the bottom of the floor.

"When I got home at lunch time these were on my steps. Vanessa, let me ask you something. When you were pregnant, was that my baby or was it his? You better tell me the truth."

"It was yours. I put that on everything, that was your baby. I am not going to lie about that."

"Oh really? Are you telling me the truth?"

"I swear I am, baby." Vanessa cried heavily.

"Vanessa, tell me the truth, did you have an abortion?" Darren stood there holding her face tightly.

"Baby, you know I had a miscarriage. I swear, Darren," Vanessa said scarily.

"You see, everything always comes to the light. I want you to take a look at this last picture. It is you going to an abortion clinic three blocks from here."

"Darren, baby." Vanessa tried to grab his arm.

"You just lied to me about three times. You know I don't like liars but you did it anyway. You did it right in my face. You know what? Get the fuck out of my house right now! You're a fucking hoe. If you wanted to be with him, you should have just been with him. Why the fuck did you make me leave my wife for you, if you didn't want to leave him?"

"Baby, I want to be with you. You are all I want. I swear."

"I swear you better get out of my house right now." Darren walked to the door, opening it and feeling the cold air.

"I am not going anywhere. I love you, Darren."

"Oh, you are not going anywhere? You are funny. You better be glad I don't beat your eyes blue for hurting me. You cheated on me. You made me leave my wife and then you kill our baby, and you have the nerves to say you love me! Bitch, you are leaving my house right now!" Darren threw the pictures down and walked over to Vanessa, grabbing her. He grabbed her arms forcedly.

"I want you out of my house right now," he said, pushing her to the door.

She fell to the ground and Darren grabbed her by her hair and arm and dragged her to the door.

"Darren stop! You are pulling my hair! Darren stop, you are hurting me! Please Darren!" Vanessa yelled, trying to get away.

He picked her up and threw her on the ground. Vanessa scraped her knee and her right hand. She cried while Darren's next door neighbor walked outside.

"Everything is okay. She just fell down the steps while we were arguing. Go back in the house, Jim."

"Darren, how could you hurt me like this?" Vanessa tried to stand up, but she was in pain.

"Jim, go ahead and go inside buddy." Darren smiled. "Everything is okay."

Jim walked inside.

"How could I hurt you? Do you know how much I gave up for you? I gave up so much. I have alimony and two kids that I am on child support for. I did this shit for you and you didn't want to give up that no good bastard. I am a deacon and I shouldn't be cursing. I shouldn't be doing any of this shit but you know what, Vanessa? This is not over. I am going to go up there to Dallas and beat his ass. Since I can't beat your ass, someone's ass I am going to beat. You people think you can go around and live in sin and think it is cool? I better not ever see your face again, especially in church. If I do, I am going to come to your house and beat your ass too. I have spoken. Now, get the fuck off of my property." Darren walked in the house, slamming the door.

Vanessa was still pain and breathing hard, watching the cold come out of her mouth. She knew she lost a good man for a man who didn't care about her. Vanessa stood up and walked to her car. Darren opened the door and threw her divorce papers on the ground and closed the door. Vanessa cried and walked and grabbed the papers and got into her car.

She backed up and drove off. She was confused on how Darren received the pictures. She took her phone out and called Brandon. She wanted answers. The phone rung and Brandon picked up.

"Vanessa, I can't talk right now. I am getting things together in my apartment," Brandon said, carrying a box to the living room.

"Apartment? I thought you lived in Tracy's house," she said, fixing her voice from crying.

"I did but she kicked me out. I have to go, Vanessa."

"Was it because of pictures of you and me?"

Brandon placed the box down in the middle of the floor. He hesitated. "Yeah...that is exactly why. How did you know?" Brandon asked, lying.

"I just left from Darren's place and he showed me pictures of you and me from the hotel. Like, these pictures were closed up together. It showed me coming out of your apartment and everything. It showed us at the restaurant too. Do you have any idea who could have done this?"

"I might have a clue. Fuck!"

"What?"

"I think it is Chelsea. I think she is behind all of this. I think she is mad because of Cash and me, and she probably knows about us."

"Brandon, I cannot keep doing this. I mean, I can't. You have so much going on in your life right now. This is too much negativity for me. I shouldn't be going through this. I am a woman who has nothing to offer but love. I didn't have a miscarriage. Brandon, I had an abortion because I wanted us back together."

"Are you serious? I thought you lost the baby."

"No, I had an abortion. We finally had a baby together and I wanted us to be together. Brandon, the baby was yours. I told Darren it was his but it was two weeks before he tried to get me pregnant."

"Vanessa, so why did you do that? Why didn't you tell me?"

"I didn't want all of this turmoil for the baby. All this drama and bullshit, he or she shouldn't be involved through all of this. It is too much, Brandon. Darren just left me and he told me he is coming after you."

"What? For what?"

"He is mad, Brandon. He is coming for you and it is good that you are not with Tracy because he would have known where you live. As long as Tracy's ass doesn't rat, you are safe."

"Look Vanessa, I have to call you back. I have to figure some shit out, and call Chelsea and Cash and get all of this shit straight now. I know for a fact that is not my baby she is carrying. All of this shit that is going on is too close. It is someone I know that is giving away everything I do. I have to find out."

"Brandon, I am going to sign these papers and I am going to move on with my life. I'm going to move to Greensboro and start a new life. After my probation is over in a couple of months, I'm going to leave. This is too much. I want a family. I want to start over. I want a man who is going to love me. You don't love me nor does Darren. I can't keep doing this. Brandon, this is it."

"I understand. I want you to always remember Vanessa, I did love you and I was happy with you. Good luck with your life."

"Thank you, take care Brandon."

"Goodbye." Brandon hung up the phone. He knew he had to be careful but went through his phone to his contacts. He stared at Chelsea's phone number and made the call. He was going to get to the bottom of everything.

Chapter Twenty-Three

Chelsea...It's Too Good

Brandon was driving. He was on the way to Tracy's house. He picked up the phone and called her.

"Tracy, I need to get that box out of the living room and if you don't mind, I want to see my son."

"Where are you?" she asked, looking at her baby in his crib.

Brandon pulled up in the driveway. "I am in the driveway."

"Listen, he is taking a nap right now. I'm going to bring the box outside."

"Ok, but can I-"

Tracy hung up the phone. Brandon threw his phone on the passenger seat and got out of the truck. He was snugged in his Dallas Cowboys' hoodie.

Tracy opened the house door, struggling with the heavy box. Brandon rushed to grab it and place it on the ground.

"I don't know why you put it on the ground. I am going inside of the house," Tracy said, grabbing each end of her yellow and white jacket. She placed both of her legs together in her wrinkled blue jeans with her hair tied up.

237

"Tracy, wait. I just want to speak. I mean, you can't give me a five-minute conversation?"

Tracy took a deep breath. "You want five minutes? Ok. What do you have to say?"

"Listen, I want to apologize to you. I swear, I didn't mean to hurt you. I really do love you, Tracy. I want to work things out, especially for our son."

"Do not put your son into this. This has nothing to do with this. Now stop it, Brandon. You do not love me, OK. You made it very clear at the courthouse who you really love. You don't love me. You don't love my kids and as far as I am concerned, you don't love your son. If you did love us, you wouldn't have done this. You wouldn't have tried to destroy this family. A real man doesn't do this. Is there anything else you would like to say?"

"I do. I love my son," Brandon said while crying, knowing he was losing everything slowly. "I love us as a family. I am sorry, Tracy. You need to give me one chance. Give me one more chance."

"Don't give me that fake crying crap, shit. Stop right there because I have heard it before. Brandon, I want you to listen and listen good. You and this family aren't going to be one. It's over. Next, you are going on child support because I don't trust you. You better be glad we didn't get married or I would take everything you got, plus your royalties from the cowboys," she said, grabbing his hoodie. "Now, get the fuck off of my property."

"Tracy. Tracy, please don't act like this. I want us to work it out. I want to see my son. Tracy, don't do this to me right now. I need you guys."

"You don't need us. You need the Dallas Cowboys. Fuck you, Brandon." Tracy turned around and shut the door hard.

Brandon shook his head. He picked up the box and walked to the truck. He placed it inside, got in, and drove off.

He picked up his phone and started to text Tracy. He was angry that she wouldn't give him a chance and was going to put him on child support.

So, you don't want to forgive me? Why because you fucking someone else? Are you going back to your ex-husband? You think you are going to let me out of my son's life? You must be out your fucking mind. I am a Dallas Cowboy bitch. I was there for you and your fucking kids when he left you guys. Fuck you bitch?!

Brandon sent his text.

Tracy sent Brandon's hand clap emojis then her message.

Brandon, this is my last message to you so I can keep it for proof. I am moving on with my life and I want you to as well. I won't take your bashing anymore and I don't have time for it. I am tired of being unhappy and if you like it then you can do it by yourself. Don't bring me and my family into your b.s. you have going on. You know what, maybe all this

happened for a reason. A lesson, you know. For you to think that every woman is a hoe on the road. Karma is going to be a bitch Brandon. I am not your wife. She might put up with your shit but not me. Maybe you should work on that issue, but first, you will have to meet karma. Now Brandon, if you keep going, I will call the cops. That is my last warning. Have a good playoff game on Sunday.

Brandon tried to crush his phone. He was upset driving home. He had no one. He knew karma was coming for him. Brandon pulled up to his driveway. He got out and walked inside of the house, placing the box down. He looked at the many boxes inside of his apartment. He went to the kitchen and got a glass of water. He had so much on his mind and he couldn't focus on the game.

He sat down with a drink of water and the doorbell rang. He got up and walked to the door. He opened it and it was Chelsea.

"Who needs a house warming gift when you have good pussy at the door?" she asked, opening up her trench coat and showing her naked body with black heels on. Chelsea had gotten thicker and her hair was in ponytails, like Brandon liked it.

Brandon smiled. "You got here fast from Houston."

"That is what good dick will do to a bitch. She will drive fast as hell to get some good dick. I have missed you, baby. I am ready to fuck you so good. I want to taste your fat dick. I want to feel it to the back of my throat. Do you want that?" Chelsea asked, opening up her pussy's lips.

Brandon nodded his head yes rapidly. She entered the house. She saw sexual frustration in his eyes. She pushed him towards the newly painted wall. She unbuckled his khakis, pulled them down to his ankles, and began sucking his dick. She spits on her hand and began stroking and sucking his dick until he started to grow. Brandon moaned. She cuffed his balls with his long dick shooting straight to her cheek.

"Do you miss me?" she asked, taking the dick out of her mouth and sucking on his balls.

Brandon looked towards the ceiling. He couldn't talk. Deep breaths came out of his soul. "Oh my God, yes, I do," he said with his toes curling inside his tan squared dress shoes.

"I thought so." Chelsea started to suck again and swiveled her head fast. Brandon's knees buckled. She began to suck his soul through his dick.

"Look at me," she said, looking into her eyes. "Does that feel good Brandon?"

"Yes baby." He looked down into her eyes.

"You want some of this pussy?"

"Fuck, yes I do."

Chelsea stopped sucking with saliva coming out of her mouth. She put it on his dick and grabbed it. She stood up and took her trench coat off. Her thighs, booty, and tits grew thicker. She bent all the way over touching her heels.

"Come get this pussy, nigga."

Brandon wanted to wear a condom because he didn't know what she was up to. He stared at her fat ass. He wanted it.

"You act like you scared of this pussy." She shook her ass, and Brandon walked up and slid in.

She moaned while gripping her ankles tighter.

"Damn nigga, that long thick dick still good. Fuck me nigga."

Brandon smacked her ass and pounded her harder. "This pussy still good." He growled with his toes curling in his shoes. He took his white dress shirt and threw it on the floor. "Throw that ass and fuck me good." Brandon drilled her.

Chelsea's tight pussy had him ready to cum.

"This pussy is too good. I have to cum already."

"Daddy, you know where I want warm cum?"

"In your mouth, right?" he asked, breathing hard and stroking fast.

"That's right, daddy, in my muthafucking mouth."

"Come get it." Brandon pulled out and held his dick until Chelsea got on her knees. He jacked it and a hot load went on her face. She spread his babies all around her face.

Brandon was out of breath. Chelsea stood up.

"Can I go wash your babies off of my face?"

"Yes, you can. The bathroom is in my bedroom. Go straight and it is on the left."

She grabbed her trench coat and walked to the bathroom with her heels clicking. Brandon followed her. He knew he was going to fuck her all night. He walked into the bedroom taking his shoes and pants off. He wanted to question Chelsea about the pictures and did she have anything to do with them. The pussy was too good. He was going to wait until the next morning and get all of this pussy he could from her.

Chapter Twenty-Four

I'm Wifey Bitch... Remember that...

The next morning at five, Chelsea woke up lying on Brandon's chest. After having sex throughout the night, she was happy. Her naked body against his body was all she wanted. She knew she had drained his balls and fucked him good. She didn't get him to cum in her again, but she wanted him to. This time, she knew she had Brandon. She flinched her body, so Brandon could wake up. He tossed a little and woke up.

"Good morning, gorgeous," Brandon said, kissing her on the lips. He patted and gripped her luscious booty.

"Good morning, baby. How did you sleep?" She tilted her head to look at him.

Brandon laughed. "We just went to sleep like an hour an ago. Naw, I'm good. I am ready for the playoff game and with the goodies you just gave me; I know we are going to win." He kissed her again.

Chelsea blushed. "That's right, baby. This is your pussy."

"Oh, is it? Thanks for telling me baby." Brandon rubbed her booty.

Brandon had morning wood and Chelsea felt it on her stomach. "Morning wood I see." Chelsea looked at it, wanting to suck it. "You want me to suck it?" Chelsea asked, pulling the sheets off of them.

He locked eyes with her and said yes.

Chelsea adjusted herself to the right side of him and slowly moved her head to his dick. Her lips were inches from sucking it. "I think you should go freshen up. You were sweating a lot and I don't want to suck salty balls and dick," she said, sitting up in the bed.

Brandon smiled. "I was sweating like Shaq. Ok, I'm going to do that. I'll be back."

Brandon got out of bed and went to the bathroom. Chelsea instantly moved to the right side of the king bed. She grabbed his phone off of the wooden nightstand. She wanted to fuck Brandon all night because she always noticed that Brandon never locked his phone until night time. She got it and went to Brandon's contacts to Vanessa and dialed her number. She placed it back on the nightstand. Brandon came out of the bathroom holding his fat dick. The phone rung and Chelsea twirled her finger for Brandon to come get her pussy. He rushed in the bed and slid inside of her.

He grabbed both legs and punished her missionary style. Chelsea shouted and moaned loudly.

"Oh God yes, fuck me Brandon! Damn, this dick feels good!"

She didn't know if Vanessa answered or not, so she wanted to be loud so she could hear. Vanessa picked up and heard Chelsea screaming. She couldn't figure out what was going on and who it was until she heard the loud moans. Vanessa shook her head and couldn't believe Brandon would do this after what she told him.

She hung up and went back to sleep. Brandon looked to the right and saw his phone lit up.

"Shit, I think someone called me." He stopped stroking.

"No, baby, don't stop. I was about to cum." She grabbed his face and kissed him. Brandon kept stroking her. Chelsea knew she was on the phone or had just hung up. She smiled while being stroked. Brandon laid on her with the side of his face on the bed. She wrapped her hands around his back and let him fuck her pussy. She didn't have to worry about Vanessa anymore.

Brandon started to pump fast. "I have to cum."

"Cum inside of baby. You know you want too." Chelsea whispered into his ear.

Brandon's face became alert and he had to cum. He slid out and came on her stomach. Chelsea was highly upset that he didn't cum inside of her.

"Why didn't you cum inside of me? Chelsea asked, looking at his babies.

Brandon got out of bed to go get her a rag from the bathroom. "I don't want any kids right now," he said, throwing her a brown rag.

She got it and wiped herself off. "That's b.s. Brandon. I want a baby. I want to be your wife."

"Chelsea, we're not even together. We just fucked. I haven't seen you in a long time."

"I don't understand. You don't want me to have your baby because we'd just seen each other, but it is okay to fuck?"

"You don't understand."

"Help me understand. Oh, I get it, this was just a fuck? So I was just a piece of pussy before the game?"

"I am not saying that. You are always assuming shit. What I am saying is I don't want to rush it?"

"You wanted to fuck me?"

"And you wanted to fuck me too, Chelsea. Stop acting like it was just me that wanted to fuck."

"Brandon, you must want to go back to your wife?"

"What? No, I don't want to be with her. She cheated on me. What the hell do I look like?"

"I am tired of you lying to me. Brandon, I saw you at the restaurant with her. You are back with her. I know you are, you fuckin' liar."

"You saw what you wanted to see, but we are not together."

"Then what was that? Go ahead and lie to me again."

"The reason why we were together was because I was trying to get her to sign the divorce papers. That's it."

"You must think I am dumb?"

"Dumb? Hell no, especially not after that plan you, Cash, and Star did. I mean that was a hell of plan. You are very smart," he said, smiling and getting back into bed.

"Whatever."

"They are signed, Chelsea. She signed them and I am a free man. I am a single man. I mean, look around. I have boxes and shit. What does that tell you?"

"Seriously?" she questioned, placing her back against the headboard. She was happy.

"Yes, but so much is going on in my life right now, and I have to focus on the game. I have to go ahead and get dressed baby. I have to be there at 8 and the game is at 4:30 pm."

"What is going on with your life?" Chelsea asked with concern.

"We will have to talk about it after the game. I have to get down there in an hour." He kissed her on the cheek. "Let me go ahead and get ready for work." He slid out of bed. "Where do you work now?"

"I am still unemployed right now. It is kind of hard, after my record."

"Yeah, I am so sorry about that. How are you living?"

"I have money saved up, so I am cool for a couple of months."

"Cool. I am about to take my shower, so I will be back. Are you going to stay or leave?"

"I might be gone. I want to get back home."

"I got you… just lock the bottom lock."

"Ok baby."

Brandon walked into the bathroom to take a shower.

Chelsea crawled on the bed to look at his phone. She saw that Vanessa answered the phone. She smiled. She opened the drawer to the nightstand and saw a black pen. She wrote down Vanessa's phone number on her arm. She placed his phone back and the black pen in the correct position. She got out of bed, got her trench coat, and put her heels on. She started to walk out of his bedroom. She looked around to make sure she didn't forget anything and walked out of the house. Brandon heard the door close and walked out.

"Chelsea? Baby? Are you here? Good." Brandon walked over to his phone and noticed that he didn't lock it. "Shit!" He checked to see if someone called and noticed Vanessa was the last person he talked to.

He didn't look at the time nor did he see it was an outgoing call. He placed it back down and went to go shower to get ready.

Chelsea backed out of the driveway and headed back to Houston. She got out of her phone and looked at her arm to get Vanessa's number. She dialed and it rung. After two rings, Vanessa answered the phone, very sleepy.

"Hello? Who is this?" Vanessa asked with a deep voice

"Eww, bitch, fix your voice. Bitch, this is the new wife. I told you that I was going to be with Brandon, whether you were dead or alive."

"Chelsea, is this you?"

"You damn right, bitch, it is."

"How did you? You know what. I know you called me to hear you fuck him and I really don't care."

"Bitch, whatever, I won. You do care."

"No, I don't care. Chelsea, what did you win baby? You are so dick whipped that you don't even know everything that is going on. You can't possibly know."

"Bitch, what are you talking about?" Chelsea gripped the steering wheel tighter.

"Chelsea, in this game he is playing, no one wins. I was his wife for a long time. We had love, real love, and you know just because I couldn't get pregnant or he couldn't keep his dick in his pants, that's why it is over. What makes you think he isn't going to cheat or commit?"

"Because I can have kids. I can give him what he wants."

Vanessa laughed. "Bitches like you are so dumb. He has a child by my ex-boyfriend's mother. He just had this baby not too long ago. You see, you don't know anything. His life is messed up. Matter of fact, my boyfriend is coming down to fight him because he found out we fucked after that night at the restaurant. You need to leave him alone and get yourself together. I know you have something to do with those pictures and you know what? I am not even mad about the situation anymore because the whole time I was thinking I had a good man; I didn't. I want to thank you for releasing that demon out of my life. Both of them, now, I have to get ready for work. I wish you well."

Tears came down Chelsea's face. "Wait? Can I have your ex-boyfriend's number, if you don't mind?

"Why? You know what, I'll text it to you. I don't know what you are up to but we haven't talked and I am not a part of your plan. But, I will give you his whereabouts, so hopefully you can dig up where Brandon might live. I want both of these bastards to pay and I know you can make that happen."

"I can, and I am sorry for the shit you and I had in the past. I am sorry about that."

"It is ok now. You made me know my worth and Chelsea, hopefully in due time, you will know yours. This is our last time talking. I will text you all the details. You never heard from me. Goodbye."

Vanessa hung up. Chelsea cried. She felt the phone vibrate. It was a text from Vanessa. She couldn't believe Brandon played her again. She wiped her tears and knew she had a plan for Brandon to fuck him up.

"OK....OK...you have baby with another bitch. Karma is going to be a bitch, Brandon, and I am going to deliver her to you."

Chapter Twenty-Five

Chelsea's At It Again

The next couple of days, Chelsea was still grieving about the things Vanessa told her about Brandon. She had a plan ready to execute. It was Sunday evening and the city of Dallas was mourning the Cowboys losing their game. They lost by three points by the team trailing 14 points. She knew Brandon's life was a wreck. Chelsea sat in one of the classiest places in Dallas. She crossed her legs at the bar of Diamonds Restaurant. She was dazzled in her favorite "catch a man" black tight dress. Her hair was straight down, and she wore a little eyeliner and six inch heels. Her phone rung and it was a number she didn't recognize. She picked up.

"Hello," Chelsea spoke nervously.

"Good evening, hi, is this Chelsea Johnson?" The older woman spoke with authority.

"Yes ma'am, this is me. Who is this?" Chelsea spoke with concern.

"Hi, yes. This is Shirley Harris from Harris Marketing Company. I looked over your resume and I must say, very impressive."

Chelsea started to get excited. "Well, thank you very much."

"Yes, I am trying to understand why you became a flight attendant with such a high grade point average?"

Chelsea laughed. "Well, I tried to get hired by a marketing company, but no one wanted me at the time. I don't know if I was thinking too big or too small at the time, so I became a flight attendant."

"Well, Ms. Johnson, a 3.8 GPA at Georgia Tech, that is very impressive. I want to schedule you an interview if you are still interested?"

Chelsea saw Darren take his seat a couple of booths down from the bar. He wore a blue sport jacket, blue jeans, a tan shirt and tan dress shoes. She knew it was him by pictures Vanessa sent her. She smiled while he looked into the menus.

"Ms. Johnson, are you there?"

"I am so sorry. Yes, I would love that." Chelsea gained focus.

"Okay, we will fund you a plane ticket? Are you still Houston?"

"Yes ma'am, I am," Chelsea said with excitement.

"Okay, great. I want you to be here in a week on Monday at 10:00 am. We will have a limousine as well."

"Wow, you treat your employees like the president."

"Ms. Johnson, we only accept the best. I am very aware of the criminal background record. If it was drugs or something extreme, I wouldn't have called you, but protecting yourself from someone's wife, I understand. I have been there and when you come here, there will be temptation. Ms. Johnson, here we have forms for everyone to sign if they are going to take that path. I will get my assistant on your information and we will speak soon."

"Thank you again," Chelsea said, smiling at Darren looking her way.

"You are welcome, Ms. Johnson, have a nice day."

Chelsea was happy but didn't want to burst out of happiness. Darren got out of his seat and walked over. She loved chocolate and didn't expect Darren to be so fine. He grabbed the seat.

"Is someone seating here?" Darren's nice breeze of cologne hit her face.

"Well, you just sat down, so a big strong guy like yourself wouldn't care if someone did. I don't think they are going to want it back now. No, no one is sitting there." Chelsea crossed her legs so Darren could see under her dress. They shook hands.

"My name is Darren Franklin and you are?"

"My name is Stephanie Greene."

"It is really nice to meet you, Ms. Greene. I was looking over there and I was saying to myself, you look very familiar. It is like I saw you somewhere before."

Chelsea knew it had to be at his church. The time she came to the church to spy on Brandon. She spoke with alarm. "No, I never saw a fine man like yourself here in Dallas."

Darren blushed while smiling. "I am from this way but I live in Atlanta now. I want to move back home but I don't think this would be a good place for me right now."

"Why do you say that?"

"Well, I just found out my girlfriend cheated on me with one of the coaches from the Cowboys."

"I am so sorry to hear that. Let me guess, is it Brandon?"

"Yes, how did you know?" Darren's fist balled up.

"Well, he has slept with a lot of women around here. I was a cheerleader for the team. One night him and I were talking, we got a little drunk, and slept together. Now, this was recent. He told me about some woman name Vanessa. I think it is an ex-wife or something. He was bragging about how he fucked her while she had a man. He was saying like once a husband's pussy, always a husband's pussy. After I heard his foul mouth, I left. If he is talking about his woman and other women like that, then he was going to talk about me. I was actually falling for this guy. I mean, he thinks he can go around doing that to women." Chelsea faked as if she was hurt.

"That son of a bitch. I wanted to marry that woman. I left my ex-wife for her because we had something special."

"I am so sorry to hear that, Darren. I mean, I know I may be getting too personal. You don't know me and I don't know you, but why did you leave your wife?"

Darren placed both hands together. The male, white young bartender walked over. "Would you two like anything to drink?"

"Yes, can you get me and this young gorgeous woman a screw driver? Is that fine?" Darren asked to make sure.

"Yes, it is."

"Okay, I will be back with your drinks," the bartender said and walked away.

"Now, back to your question." Darren cleared his throat.

"This sounds like it is going to be really good." Chelsea pulled out her little mirror from her pocketbook.

"My ex-wife and I have two gorgeous kids together. I was with her but I wasn't with her. I always wanted Vanessa before she got married to Brandon. I remember I saw her at the family reunion when I was with Tracy before and this woman made my heart melt. She was pure gold. She is a classy woman. I wanted to be her everything but we were with two different people. I was a deacon here and I told my wife one day that I didn't love her. We pretty much went our separate ways. I got into a church as a deacon where Vanessa was and bam. There were many sequences of events after that, but after I found that out. I have to find him for causing this pain. I left my kids and my ex-wife to be with her and this is what he does to me. He has to pay. I am going to find out where he lives. I am only going to be here until Tuesday. I have to find him. I am going to beat his ass."

Chelsea smiled. "I like your plan. I think karma is going to hurt him really bad," she said, receiving her drink.

"Oh, it's going to hurt, especially when I kick his ass," Darren said, holding his glass for a toast.

"Cheers," Darren said as they knocked glassed together. "But, enough about that fool. Tell me Ms. Greene, why is a gorgeous woman, like yourself, in a restaurant by yourself?"

"Because all of the good men, like yourself, are taken."

"I am not taken at all, but I am very interested into getting to know you."

"Darren, I am going to be honest with you. This is something I do not do but I have to do."

"What is it?"

"I want to be a slut tonight." Chelsea said, licking her lips.

Darren spit out his drink over the bar. He coughed and Chelsea laughed. "Excuse me," Darren said while coughing.

She giggled. "I am sorry." She patted him on the back.

"No, no, it is fine. You want to be a slut tonight?"

"I am very straight forward and I want to be fucked tonight. Is that something you can do?"

Darren smiled. "Umm…yes…I can do that for you."

"Great because we both are getting over someone and I think we need a little fun."

Darren licked his lips. "You are right about that."

"My room is right across the street here, at the Hilton. It is 114. You can walk me over there if you are okay and don't worry. I have condoms."

"Well, what are we waiting here for? Hey, my man, here is the damages for the drinks," he said, getting out of the booth and paying the bartender.

Chelsea got out of as well and they both walked out of the door. Darren lingered back to check out Chelsea's ass. They walked across the street to the hotel.

"After you finish fucking me, I am going to give you Brandon's address. I know where he lives."

"He doesn't live with my ex-wife?" Darren scratched his head.

"I guess not or he might have a fuck spot, but who cares, as long as you get him, right?'

"You are so right gorgeous," Darren said, wanting to take her clothes off. "Maybe, after you are rested up, after being fucked good, you can go beat his ass. But it is going to be a long night. It is already 9 pm. I want you to spend the night," Chelsea said, stopping at her room door.

"I am going to do that. Deacons don't get put in jail."

Chelsea opened the door and they walked in. They got around the corner to see the bedroom and saw Star playing with her pussy in the bed while licking her fingers.

"Deacon Darren, I hope you don't mind if it is two of us, do you?" Chelsea asked, walking over to the bedroom and taking off her dress."

"Damn. Well praise the Lord," Darren said, smiling to the skies.

Chelsea got in the bed with her on all fours and Star began eating her pussy from the back. Chelsea moaned while looking at Darren. Star smacked her ass and spread her cheeks. Her long tongue and hot breath made Chelsea's pussy wetter.

Star stopped eating. "Nigga, are you going to come fuck or what? You have two bad bitches naked. Take off all of your clothes and come fuck us." Star laid back while Chelsea lied flat on the king size bed, eating her pussy. Star ran her fingers through Chelsea's hair. Darren smiled and took his clothes off.

"Shit...Stephanie, that is right, eat that pussy. Damn nigga, you have a long dick. You are a sexy man. Come stick that fat dick in my mouth."

Darren walked over. He got in the bed on his knees, and Star grabbed his dick and received it in her mouth. Her mouth was wet and hot. Darren closed his eyes. Chelsea stopped eating her and crawled to lick his balls. Darren moaned and couldn't believe what was going on.

"Let's sit this big dick nigga down," Star said with drool coming out of her mouth. Darren sat down on the bed. Each woman was on the side of him lying down, shaking their asses and sucking his dick. Darren's ten inches was rock hard and ready to fuck.

"Girl, I want to fuck this chocolate nigga first," Star said. She got on her knees and got on top of him.

Darren didn't even think about a condom. He didn't want to mess the mood up.

"Girl, you can have him." Chelsea got up and sat down in the chair. She spread her legs with her feet on the chair, playing with her pussy. She watched Star ride Darren's long dick. Her fat ass bounced. Chelsea grabbed her phone and took a picture. She sent it to Vanessa. Chelsea send her text.

You have proof, just in case he wanted you back. He has fucked my homegirl Star. Whatever you do....do not fuck him because he is fucking raw and she has vaginal herpes. She got it from one of the college football players in Houston. His karma has finally caught up with him, girl.

Vanessa texted him back. **Good and thank you.**

Darren got off of her and started to fuck Star from the back.

"Are you coming to fuck?" Darren asked, sliding into Star while she grabbed the sheets.

"I am just going to watch. I wanted to be a slut but I want to watch her fuck you."

"Fuck me nigga, don't worry about her," Star said, throwing her ass back at him.

After many minutes, Darren had to cum. "Damn, you have so good pussy. You are going to make me cum."

"Go ahead and cum daddy," Star said with her eyes closed.

"That is a shame, all of that big dick going to waste," Chelsea whispered to herself.

Darren slid out and Star got up and caught Darren's cum. She continued to suck and jack until all of his nut was gone.

"How was that, Darren?" Chelsea asked, getting up and gathering his things.

"That was good. She has some good ass pussy," Darren said, looking at her throwing his clothes on the bed.

"I am sorry Darren, but I have an interview tomorrow. I got a call and I have to drive back to Houston," Chelsea paused, waiting for him to put on his clothes.

Darren got his things and started putting his clothes on.

"Hey, but you did a great job fucking me." Star got up, heading to the bathroom and winking at Chelsea.

"Thanks. Well, congrats on your job offer. You think I can get your number?"

"I'd rather not. You can get her number if you would like. I am sorry." Chelsea went to write down Brandon's information.

"Ok," Darren said with confusion. "So, what just happened here?"

"You just got some pussy while I watched." She handed him the information. "Here is Brandon's information. I am just getting over him, but if we see each other next time, then I will give you my number and we will go from there. Faith, right?" Chelsea gave him a hug.

Darren hugged her. "That is right."

"You have a nice night." She walked Darren to the door.

"You as well." Darren walked out of the room.

Chelsea smiled. She knew she got Darren and next was Brandon.

"Star, pack your bags. It is time to head back to Houston. That nigga might be crazy and come back."

Chapter Twenty-Six

Time to Face Karma

The next day after the disappointing lost the Cowboys suffered, Brandon was in his office getting the things he didn't want to leave in his office. He grabbed the box and walked out of the office and the facility. He got into his truck and decided to drive to Coach Carter's house. Everyone, from the owner to the football players, was mad with him because of the call he called to make them lose. He and Coach Carter were good friends since he has been in Dallas. Brandon arrived to Coach Carter at 2:04 pm on a Monday, a cold day in Dallas. He parked and saw Coach Carter's car in the driveway. He got out wearing a grey hoodie and grey sweat pants. He walked to the door and knocked. No one answered the door, so he rang the doorbell. Coach Carter came to the door half-naked in his Dallas Cowboy's shorts.

"Hey Brandon, what's up man?" Coach Carter asked, opening the door up a little.

"Hey man, are you okay?" Brandon sounded concerned, while trying to peek inside.

"Yeah man, I am doing great, man. I'm just cleaning up, that's all."

"Okay, I came to holla at you man. I wanted to talk about this game, if you didn't mind."

"You know what, man? I am kind of cleaning here and-" he said nervously.

"Man, watch out." Brandon pushed the door open.

Brandon walked in and seen a lot of things gone from the house. The house was almost empty.

"Are you moving or something? Did they fire you?" Brandon asked, walking to the living room. The only thing he saw was a 60-inch flat plasma TV.

"Naw man, my wife left me, man. She has been gone since that time I told you at the restaurant. She took everything and went to work for an engineering company in Europe," Coach Carter said, almost about to shed a tear.

"Damn man, I didn't know that. Why didn't you let me know?"

"I couldn't man. I didn't want to show any type of weakness. I am kind of private and this hurt me really bad, man. I mean, fuck, why did she have to leave man?" Coach Carter started to cry and Brandon gave him a hug.

"What happened man? She didn't just leave like that?"

"I…I got caught fucking a girl. She came home and came into my man cave and saw this broad riding my dick. When she came to move, she called the cops and I couldn't be within 100 feet from her while she moved. It was crazy man. I love my wife but damn, she is about to get me for everything man. She took a lot. I don't have shit. That is why I have been partying and fucking like crazy because I am trying to keep my mind off of her. She was my everything."

"It is going to be okay, you just have to grow from this. You have to win her back."

"I can't man."

"Why do you say that?"

Coach Carter walked to the table in the living room and grabbed his phone and threw it to Brandon.

"Take a look."

Brandon looked at the phone and saw that his wife had a new lover.

"She is already in a relationship. I fucked up, Brandon. I like fucking these young bitches but I don't love it. She never wanted to have kids with me because she said I wasn't ready. I wasn't ready to be a dad because I wasn't a good husband. I wasn't a real man."

"Listen, man, you're going to have to man up and when you find the woman who is right for you, you will love her like she is supposed to be loved. I wish I could have known that from my wife. You know I was out here fucking these hoes like Chelsea, Cash, and the rest of chicks, but I love my wife."

The back room door closed.

"You have someone here?" Brandon asked, looking back towards the hall.

"You know it. I told you man. I can't stop fucking them." Coach Carter laughed in spirits. "But no Brandon, I do miss her, but she is not coming back. I am going to have to suck it up, man."

"You ain't shit." Brandon laughed and gave Coach Carter a hi-five.

"That is right. Now, let me get my back, so I can get me a nut."

"Nothing wrong with that." Brandon started walking back to the door. "Do you think they are going to fire me, man?"

"You are safe man. You got this. So what we lost in the first round but before you last year, we were 8-8. Man, you are good. Don't worry."

"I really appreciate that man. I will get with you later. I have to figure all of this shit out."

"Me as well." Coach Carter opened the door and let Brandon out.

Brandon walked to his truck, got in, and drove off. He looked in his phone and seen a message from a strange number.

Special delivery. I hope you like a little taste of karma. It is time for you to meet it. You are a sorry ass man and a sorry ass Coach. I hope the Cowboys drop you. Goodbye!

Brandon put his phone down. He thought it was a threat message because of the game. He didn't care because he knew they were coming. He started to think about everything. He really wanted to call Vanessa. He wanted to see his son. Many thoughts were going through his head. He pulled up to his apartment complex. He got out of the truck and started to walk to the door and was punched in the back of the head. He fell to the ground and felt punches and kicks in the back."

"You piece of shit! I am going to fuck you up," Darren said, punching him in the back of the head.

Brandon tried to get in position to fight back but Darren was too strong. Darren flipped him to the other side and Brandon threw a punch back that gave him time to get back on his feet. Brandon threw another punch in Darren's face but he grabbed his hand and picked up Brandon by the throat and slammed him on the concrete.

"God may forgive but I don't. I am going to fuck you up," Darren said, punching Brandon in the face repeatedly. His face bruised up. He became unconscious as Darren continued to punch him until blood came from his mouth and his eye was swollen shut. Darren stopped.

"Lord, please forgive me. You son of a bitch. You better stay away from Vanessa or next time, you won't have eyes to see. You piece of shit." Darren spit on him and walked back to his car.

Brandon laid there not moving. An elderly woman came out of her apartment and saw Brandon on the ground. She screamed for her grandson to call the police and she stood by Brandon's side until the ambulance came.

Chapter Twenty-Seven

Time For The Truth

Brandon was in the hospital on i.v.'s. He finally woke. When he opened his eyes, he saw Cash and Coach Carter sitting down in the chairs in the room.

"He is waking up," Cash said, standing up and checking on Brandon.

"Hey buddy. Are you okay?" Coach Carter asked, standing up on the other side of the bed.

"Where am I?" Brandon opened his eyes up slowly. He was dressed in a hospital gown with bruises all over his face.

"You are in the hospital. You have been in a coma for about three days now. They said an old woman saw you on the ground bleeding. Do you know how this happened?" Coach Carter asked, looking at how bruised he was.

Brandon spoke slowly. "All I remember was being hit from behind. I tried to fight back but I couldn't. The dude was so strong."

"Do you know who did it?"

"I do, but I am not going to say. I am going to let him have this one."

"Buddy, I think you should turn this guy in. I mean, you have been in a coma for three days, buddy. No one had any idea when you were going to wake up."

Brandon tried to sit up. "I am good Coach Carter. Cash, what are you doing here?" Brandon noticed that her stomach had gotten bigger. "You really are pregnant, aren't you?"

Cash laughed. "Yes, I told you I was Brandon. I wasn't lying."

"Cash, listen, I want to say I am really sorry for what I did to you. I really did like you, but I was in a terrible situation. Now, with everything that happened, I am sorry about all of it. I will be there to take care of my child. I promise I will and if you want to give us another shot, I will consider it. Thanks for being by my side." Brandon smiled while looking at her.

"That is really nice of you Brandon, but I am good," Cash said, moving from the left side of the bed rail to stand next to Coach Carter.

"What do you mean?" Brandon watched Coach Carter put his arm around Cash. "Wait, what the fuck is going on here?"

"Hey buddy, you are too weak to move. You just need to rest," Coach Carter said, giving Cash a kiss.

"I don't know who beat your ass, but they tried to kill you and Brandon, if I was smart, I think Chelsea had something to do with this. Or that is what happens when you are a sorry ass coach," Cash said laughing.

"Did you two have something to do with this?" Brandon tried to gain strength but couldn't.

"What part do you want to know, guy?" Coach Carter asked, letting Cash go and putting both hands on the bed rail.

"Did you have something to do with me getting into a fight?"

"Fight, no. I didn't plan that at all, but the rest, yes." Coach Carter let the rail go and started to walk around the room slowly. "You see Brandon; everything was a set up from the beginning. Your punk ass had to become a Cowboy at the wrong time. You came at the time when they were considering me as the defensive coordinator. I was finally going from Defensive Back Coach to Defensive Coordinator but when you came and got the job, I was hurt. I should have gotten that position. I had more track record than you, you piece of shit. For months, I pretended to be your fucking friend. I didn't give a fuck about you. You cost me my wife. She left me because I didn't make enough money. I promised her that I would if I got that position. She gave me one week, but when you came in and got the position, she left. She took all of it. What did I have to give her, Brandon? Not a Goddamn thing!" Coach Carter yelled until he was red.

"Baby, chill," Cash said, trying to calm him down. "So, what happened was when I was coming for you with the plan that Chelsea had, I saw Coach Carter in the same restaurant a week and half before I met you. We talked, we fucked, and we began a great relationship. He was telling me about his wife and how he wanted to get you back as well. I did everything to get close to you by using him. Chelsea wanted you and I did too, but once I figured you weren't going to be real with me, I made myself his woman. He gave me all the information where you were. That night when I heard you were with your wife, I knew from that day forward, I was going to make you pay."

"How did I pay? What did you do to make me pay?" Brandon asked angrily.

"Well, by the pictures," Coach Carter said, breathing hard. "Brandon, I was everywhere and I was with their friend, Star. When you went to DR I was there as well, but we had so many disguises, you didn't recognize me. When you went to the hotel with Vanessa, I was down in the next room and we took pictures of you going in and since we are coaches for the Dallas Cowboys, I was able to sneak a camera inside of your room. We had the pictures, man. We had all the information to fuck your relationship up with Tracy, things that would upset Chelsea, and things with Vanessa. We were a step ahead of all those bitches."

Cash walked up to Brandon's face. "This isn't your baby. It is his. I was trying to see if I would able to get any money from you, but now since this has happened, our plan is done."

"What the fuck do you mean?" Brandon asked, looking at them both.

"Don't curse at my lady." Coach Carter cleared his throat. "Well, this is what, your third fuck up? You know you don't get that many being a Cowboy."

"I was jumped. How is this my fault? Plus, this is number two?"

"Baby-"

Cash pulled out her phone. "The videos of us at the restaurant went viral. Plus, I sent a video of you smacking me. Oh, check this out. I did a little of editing to it."

Cash played the video of her and Brandon fucking and smacking her in the face.

"You are not going anywhere, you fucking bitch. I am a Dallas Cowboy. Fuck you." Brandon slapped her again. Cash put her phone away.

"You told me to smack you." Brandon had his mouth opened. He knew his life was all over.

"I had a camera in your room that night as well. You were a Dallas Cowboy, but once you get out of this hospital, you won't be. I have already gotten a voicemail about the position. Karma is a bitch, isn't it," Coach Carter said while laughing. "Baby, do you have anything else to say to him?"

"Yes." Cash spit in his face.

Brandon tried to sit up and hit her but couldn't.

"Hit her if you want to. I will record you and beat your ass." Coach Carter pulled her away. "Enjoy the unemployment line." He opened the door and they both walked out of the door.

Brandon started to cry. He knew karma had caught him. He had no one by his side. The doctor walked in to check on Brandon. He wanted to make sure Brandon was okay to check out. He discharged him the next day. Once Brandon was released from the hospital, he had to take a cab home. His phone was dead. Brandon couldn't wait for his phone to charge up, so he could call the general manager to explain everything to him. The cab pulled up to his apartment complex. Brandon paid the cab driver and got out and made his way to his apartment slowly. He got his keys out, opened the door, and walked in.

He slowly walked in heading to his bedroom. He placed the phone on the charger and sat on the edge of the bed. He powered it on and saw he had two voicemails and fifteen texts messages. He went through his texts messages and saw different numbers that were death threats from fans of the Cowboys. He saw Chelsea sent him a text message. He opened the message up and read it.

LOL...Karma is a bitch isn't it. You see Brandon...I am the bitch that you don't want to fuck with. I am the woman that should have been your wife, but I am leaving. I have learned my worth. You are nothing. None of you men are anything. The guy Darren who beat your ass did a good job. How do I know, because I saw you in the hospital? I just looked at you and laughed. He whupped your ass. I told him where you lived. I spotted him in a restaurant. I remembered him from church and he was looking for you. Hey, don't try to get revenge either because he fucked Star and guess what? Star has herpes. I am guessing that he is bumped up and burning like hell right now. You niggas think ya'll can fuck up

women's lives and get away. I am the wrong bitch to fuck with. You do not fuck with bitches like me. You keep screaming you're a Cowboy but that dumb bitch Cash didn't think I didn't know what her and that white boy had up their sleeves. I always know what is going on. I am that bitch. I am leaving. I am done with you Brandon. I am done with niggas like you. I know there is a guy that is going to accept me and help change my ways. Enjoy life because Karma has met you. Bye.

Brandon shook his head and sucked his tongue. He went to his voicemail and pressed 1.

"Fuck you Coach Williams. I am a mad fan."

Brandon pressed 7. He went to the next message.

"Mr. Williams, this is Jerry Frazier, the owner of the Cowboys. We have received a video, we seen the viral videos, we heard about the fight and more. We need you to come clean your office out. You have been resigned. Thank you."

He hung up. Brandon threw his phone hard against the wall and the back of the battery cover came out. Brandon was mad and started to cry. He knew his life was a mess. Karma had finally caught up to him…

Chapter Twenty-Eight

Doctor…Please Just Let Me Confess

Chelsea caught her flight on Friday. They paid for her to stay over the weekend to enjoy the city of Manhattan. She landed at the airport at 10:04 a.m. There was a driver and a limousine that took her to the biggest hotel in Manhattan. She knew this had to be a new start for her. She got out and got all of her belongings. She checked in and went to her room. After staying an hour, she caught a cab and headed a couple of blocks over. She paid the driver and got out to walk into Dr. Shelly Davis' office. She opened the wooden door and walked in. The old wooden floor creaked every time she walked. She signed in.

The young black attractive woman at the front desk spoke, "Hey there, are you a first time patient of Mrs. Davis?'

"Yes, I am," Chelsea said, moving her long hair from her right side of her eye.

"Ok. You are going to have to fill out this information first. After you are done, she will see you."

"Okay, thanks." Chelsea grabbed the clipboard. She walked to the many empty seats of gray chairs. Her navy blue heels clicked every time she walked the creaked floors. Her navy woman's suit was snug over her body because she was getting thicker. Before she was able to sit down, Mrs. Shelly Davis walked out. She was short, elderly, and had a wig on. She had her glasses in her hands with a black and gray woman's suit on.

"Ms. Johnson?" She questioned, walking closer to Chelsea.

"Yes ma'am," Chelsea said, sticking her hand out to shake.

"Dr. Shelly Davis." She shook her hand. "Please, come into my office," she said, directing her into the office.

Chelsea walked into the office and sat down in the gray chair. There was a wooden desk and many pictures of her clients and family hung on the wall. Chelsea gazed around the room. She saw some celebrities and saw pictures of her and her husband on her desk. Mrs. Shelly Davis sat down.

"Ms. Johnson, can I call you Chelsea?" she asked, pulling out a new folder to write down notes.

"Yes ma'am, you can. Do you want me to fill the paperwork out now?"

"You can in a minute. I know I am a psychiatrist but I am also a preacher at my church. When you were on the phone, I felt a spirit. Now, I usually do not take new patients on a Friday but God told me to see you. Now Chelsea, please tell me your story."

"Aren't we supposed to sign a confidential form first?" Chelsea asked, looking for it through the papers.

"You are right, that is the paper right there. No one will know about our conversation."

Chelsea signed it and put the clipboard on the other chair. She placed her purse down as well and took a deep breath. "Mrs. Shelly Davis, from a child, my life has not been right. It seems like all I know is pain because that is all I had growing up. When I was a child, my dad died when I was one month, from a car accident. I remember growing up and seeing my mom with different men and being beaten from different men all of her life. I am the only child, and my mom and I do not have a close relationship. I tried to get close but she shuts me out of her life. I love my mother, even though she had three of her boyfriends rape me because she was drugged up. I was fifteen years old. I lost my virginity to a guy and I didn't even know his name.

It hurt me all of my life. I got pregnant by this guy and my mom made me have an abortion. I didn't know what was going on until I got older. I was kicked out at eighteen years old, at the time I was living in Austin, Texas, and I moved to Houston where my grandma lived. For two days, I was homeless. I lived in a shelter and watched those people cold and hungry." Chelsea started to tear up.

"It is ok, Chelsea. Please, get it all out," Mrs. Shelly Davis said, giving her some tissues.

"I am sorry. I moved with my grandma. My grandma never gave up on me. I had good grades and I had scholarships to many colleges. She told me to pick a college because she was dying and told me whatever I needed, she would pay for. I told her I wanted to go to Georgia Tech and I did. I graduated at the top of my class."

"Chelsea, that is very impressive. You have been through so much. Even though your relationship with your mother didn't work out, God wanted you to fight. He made you stronger. God will move you from something and somewhere that will stop your growth to a place that will let you blossom. Chelsea, that is what he did for you."

"I understand what you are saying, but I am so hurt. Even though I am so successful, I still had a hole in my heart. My mother and our relationship still affected me. I graduated but I didn't get any job offers in my career, so I moved back to Houston and I became a flight attendant. When my grandma died, I got an inheritance of 4.3 million dollars."

"Wow, that is a lot of money."

"Yes, I used that money to chase down guys. I felt like guys was the key to my happiest. I have had sex with forty guys in four years."

"Oh Chelsea, lust is not the answer. The fact that you saw your mother with so many different men reflected your life like this. Chelsea, you have to let that spirit go. It is not worth it."

"Yes ma'am, I know. I mean, just recently, I did something harsh and the only reason I did it because I was in love with him."

"What did you do?"

"There was this guy I met and he was married. I had sex with him, but the only reason why I did it was because he said he was going to leave his wife for me."

"Chelsea, let me tell you something. When a man like that says that, 10 out of 10 times, he is lying. If he wanted out, he would have left her before he met you. You are nothing to them but a booty call. That is all you will ever be to them."

"I found that out."

"What did you do?"

"I thought he was going to leave me. I snapped. I attacked his wife on the airplane, and I went to jail and a psych ward for it."

"I saw that on the news."

"It was me. After I got out, I had a plan to make him pay. I got another girl to do some things for me, but she fell in love with him and we fought. After that, I left and came back with more plans towards him, and I had sex with him again. I wanted him to leave his wife and I called her while we were having sex so she could leave him. Come to found out, she left and she had another baby by him. Mind you, this guy messed up a happy home with her new boyfriend. I talked to her and she told me he was going to Dallas to beat him up. She told me where he was going to be at and I spotted him. We had a drink and went back to my room. I let him have sex with my home girl and she has herpes, and he didn't know and didn't wear a condom. We kicked him out and I gave him an address to the guy's house, and he beat him up so bad that he put him in a coma. I visited him in the hospital and left him a nasty text message. Before I got on the plane, I told my friend where the girl she wanted to fight lived and now, I am here. I have a job interview on Monday. Hopefully, I can start over a new leaf and go

279

to church because I need to be in the Lord's house. Mrs. Davis, that is my story." Chelsea cried into the tissues.

Mrs. Davis got out of her chair and sat down in the chair next to Chelsea. She sat on the edge, not sitting on her things.

"It is okay, Chelsea. Listen, you need to ask God for forgiveness. If you are serious about going to church, I will make sure you come to my church. I will make sure you are taken care of. Your spirit is troubled and you need to be saved. Do you love Jesus?"

"I do, but I don't know anything. I never been to church before." Chelsea looked into Mrs. Davis' eyes.

"That is okay. Do you want to accept him into your life?"

"Yes ma'am."

"Come to my church and be born again. I will take care of you, child."

"I really do appreciate it. I feel so much better talking to you right now."

"No problem. What you need to do is get in contact with your mother and try to build a better relationship with her. Is she still alive?"

"Yes, she is. She is actually getting married to a great guy in her life today at the courthouse. She texted me today."

"Well, that is great news. You see, when you have been through so much hell and you keep pushing and you place God in your life, heaven is on the way. It seems like you can make the relationship improve."

"She has tried but everything she has done makes me not want to."

"Chelsea, you have to forgive. You have forgiven everything that happened. How old was your mom when she had you?"

"She was fourteen years old."

"She was a child herself. She didn't know how to be a mother at fourteen. Everything that happened has made you stronger. You two have to forget the past and work on this relationship now. It is going to take time but one day is better than no days. Even if you have to be the bigger person, try to work on it. Once you are born again on Sunday, your heart will make you feel better."

"Yes ma'am. I really appreciate that."

"How about we go get some lunch and talk a little more?" Mrs. Shelly Davis offered, standing up.

"I would like that. Do you want me to fill the paperwork out?"

"Don't worry about it. You will be a member of my church. We are now family, Chelsea. One more thing Chelsea, you wait on God, he will send you your king at the right time. No matter if you are going through it or not, he will be right on time." Mrs. Shelly Davis grabbed her things.

"Thank you so much." Chelsea almost started to cry.

They got their stuff and walked out of the office. They left to get lunch. Chelsea had a spirit over her. She was hoping she get the job and have a new start in her life. She received a text from her mother with her new husband at the courthouse. She was hoping that her relationship with her mom would improve.

Chapter Twenty-Nine

Didn't I Tell You…

Cash moved all of her things into Coach Carter's house. She was happy with him and finally free from Brandon. She was four months pregnant with his child. Chelsea sent Cash Tracy's address. Chelsea knew Cash wanted to beat her ass. Cash looked at her cellphone while sitting on the toilet. She wiped, got up, and washed her hands. She went into the bedroom and Coach Carter was watching tv. Cash went into the closet to get a black heavy jacket.

"Where are you about to go?" he questioned her.

"I have to go do something real quick," Cash said, pulling her jeans up.

"What do you have to do, Katrina?"

"I want to go fight this chick really quick." Cash looked at him.

He turned the television off. "Katrina, you are pregnant. You shouldn't be fighting. You should be here with me. You don't need this nor does the baby."

Cash started to get upset. "I know, check this out. I have to finish what I started. She said she wanted to beat my ass."

"What is it going to solve but you going to jail? You might do something dumb and I don't want to see my child without his or her mother. So no, you are not going anywhere. You are going to stay here and we will continue to move all of your stuff in. It is not worth it." Coach Carter stood out of bed in his red briefs.

"Okay baby." Cash walked over to give him a hug. "Well, I am going to get the rest of the stuff out of my car you got me."

"Sure, you need help?"

"I don't. I will be right back."

Cash walked out, blowing him a kiss. She walked to the front door with a sneaky face. She hurried before he saw her get into the car. She ran to the drop top Camaro. Coach Carter walked out of the house yelling while she backed up.

"Katrina! Fuck!"

Cash drove to the directions that were given to her. She drove ready to fight. She pulled up to Tracy's house and pulled in the driveway. She didn't see any cars but she assumed it was in the garage. She got out of the car. Cash didn't care who was inside. She wanted to beat her ass. She got out trying to warm her hands. She walked up to the front door and rang the doorbell. No one came to the door. She rang it again. She was freezing cold outside. She turned around slowly and felt a punch in the face. She was trying to regain her position. She was kicked in the leg and fell to the ground. She was being jumped by four girls. They kicked and punched her in the face. Cash tried to fight them off but couldn't. She screamed for help. Tracy opened her window.

"Bitch, you can never trust these hoes. Your girl, Chelsea, told me you were coming." Tracy laughed. "Get this bitch off of my property." Tracy looked as they beat her.

"Make sure ya'll don't hit her in the stomach. She is pregnant. We just want this bitch to know who she is messing with."

They finally finished beating Cash and her face was a mess. Her light skin was purple and had bruised spots. Cash got up and slowly walked to the car stumbling.

"Bye bye, bitch." Tracy waved and smiled as Cash backed up and drove off.

Cash started to scream. "Fuck! Fuck!"

She grabbed her phone and started to call Chelsea's number. She called but she changed her number. She called Star and she changed her number too. Cash screamed. "You fuckin' bitch, that was some fucked up shit you did, Chelsea. I am going to find you fucking ugly bitch. After I have my baby, I am coming for you. You bitches haven't heard the last of me

Chapter Thirty

The Side Chick Who Turned Into A Wife

Chelsea had accepted The Lord and Savior into her life. She felt wonderful. She was working on building a better relationship with her mother. It was time for Chelsea's interview. She walked into the large building, went to the receptionist's desk, and let them know she was here for her interview. The building was about twenty floors and have different companies combined together. The woman at the front desk told her to have a seat and she would get her when she is ready. Chelsea sat down in her black skirt with a little slit cut in between. She had her hair in a ponytail that touched her white dress shirt. She sat there nervous with her purse. A guy walked in. He was dressed up. Chelsea gazed at his feet and worked her way up. His legs were long. He had a bulge in his gray slacks and a black Polo shirt. His biceps popped out of shirt and he was showing his pretty white teeth. His waves were deep. The woman at the front desk smiled while looking at him as he walked towards Chelsea.

He spoke, "Hi."

Chelsea was confused. "Hi."

"My name is Orlando Jones. I am sorry to creep up on you like this. I saw when you got out of the cab and what I am about to say might freak you out."

Chelsea was filled with curiosity. "My name is Chelsea, try me."

286

"I had an interview three blocks from here but something told me to walk. *Don't catch the cab here keep walking.* I walked. I obeyed then I saw you. I heard the voice of the Lord say, 'That is her'." He smiled. "You are the one. You are the woman God wants me to marry.

Chelsea started to cry.

"Mrs. Johnson, Mrs. Harris will see you now," the receptionist said.

"Go ahead and go to your interview. I will wait for you." He stood up as she did.

"Ok, I will be back." Chelsea walked off smiling.

The summer came and Vanessa was off of probation. She took the job in Greensboro Memorial Hospital. She was ecstatic. She bought a home and was setting up. She was a free woman and she wasn't doing any dating. She was happy for new beginnings. She had plenty of boxes to unpack but was really glad to have her bed set up. She started work in two days. Vanessa walked into the kitchen of her four bedroom, 2 ½ bath home. She heard a knock on the door. She walked to the door in her little green shorts and wife beater. She opened the door and it was Brandon.

"Hey." Brandon smiled with roses.

"Brandon?" Vanessa questioned with shock.

Vanessa and Brandon started to date again. Brandon became the defensive coordinator for the

Carolina Panthers. They had twins and got remarried. Brandon never cheated on her.

Chelsea got closer to her mom. Her and Orlando got married within two months. They have three kids now. They both are saved and Chelsea manages the top celebrities.

Cash and Coach Carter have two gorgeous girls. He was upset with her but forgave her. Cash never went back to fight Tracy. She listened to her husband and let her anger go.

As for Darren, he went to jail. He was caught having sex with different women, giving them herpes.

Star went back to stripping in Atlanta, Georgia and has a boyfriend. He doesn't know she has herpes. They wear a condom every time they have sex.

The End

THANK YOU FOR READING!!!

"Meet the Author"

Marques Lewis

Marques Lewis (30 years old) was born in Newark, New Jersey and raised until 12 years old in Irvington, New Jersey. Dora and James Lewis are out of Lincolnton and Shellman, Georgia. Marques and his family moved from Irvington, New Jersey in 1997 to Leesburg, Georgia. He attended Lee County High School and graduated from Darsey Private High School with 3.0 G.P.A. Marques began writing at the age of 7 years old. He wrote his first short story, Detective David: "The Missing Toy Boat."

After taking a 15 year hiatus, Marques began writing again after discovering the author Zane and her writings. From then, his imagination took off. At 22 years old Marques began writing plenty of short stories, poems, and encouraging women's self-esteem on social network sites. After gaining confidence, he began performing his poems at Chilli's Bar & Lounge at Open

Mic Night. The crowd loved him, and he began performing every Wednesday. He appeared in the Dec. 10, 2010 and April 6, 2012 publication short poem book, "The Poetic Lounge Vol. 2 and 3". His own poems "Weak" and "I Am A Woman" were selected. Marques then decided that he wanted to write novels.

Marques has written several novels "It's Love For Her" Part 1, "It's Love For Her" P art 2, "It's Love For Her" Part 3, "Words of Wetness", "Good Men Still Exist" with Author Jamila Gomez, "The Man Next Door" "The Road to the Perfect Guy" Part 1, "The Road To The Perfect Guy" Part 2, "The Road To The Perfect Guy" Part 3, The Side Chick Who Turned Into A Wife", "The Side Chick Who Turned Into A Wife" Part 2, "Married & Miserable", "The Woman Who Got Away Part 1, "The Woman Who Got Away" Part 2, "Dating Jordan", and "How's Your Stripper's D**k?", and his first relationship book, "Never Settle...Never Again".

Marques won 2013 "Best Selling Award" and was the runner-up for "Author of the Year" at One Karma Publishing Banquet in Alpharetta, Georgia. Marques has appeared as an extra football player in

Sherwood Baptist Church 2nd movie "Facing the Giants and also played a detective in "Taken 3" and also a role in a short story film "Double Film." He has appeared in Black Albany, GA Magazine in October 2012, and being the first author in "Big In Da Street Magazine" rap magazine May 18, 2013. He has been interviewed on W-ASU FM Albany State Radio station in October 2011. He has appeared in Lee County Ledger twice, Southwest Georgian, and Citizen Times, Lincoln Journal, Cuthbert Southwest Tribune, and Albany Herald newspapers. Marques were a special guest on "The Good Day Morning Show" on Fox 31 in June 10, 2013.

Marques was a featured author at Wellingtons and Wine at a Wine Tasting event in Albany, Georgia at Icons Bar Grill on November 23, 2013. On December 15, 2013 he produced his first play at his church (Church of God of Prophecy) "The Birth of Jesus Christ". Marques has signed as an author with True Glory Publications, LLC and very excited to be working with the company. Marques is excited by the many blessings that awaits him. Marques has his own publishing company called Marvelous Leaders Publications, LLC. He has signed authors and cannot wait to share their work with everyone.

You can find Marques' novels on www.amazon.com and www.goodreads.com. His novels on Kindle, the Amazon Kindle app, and paperback as well. You can add Marques on Facebook at Author Marques Lewis, Twitter, Instagram @iammarqueslewis, and his websitewww.iammarqueslewis.com. You can also reach him at his email address marques.lewis@aol.com. To submit to Marvelous Leaders Publications email your first three chapters of your manuscript, a bio of yourself, and the synopsis of yourself. Marques is always working to improve his craft. He likes to tell his fans to follow their dream, keep God first, keep the faith, and most of all don't give up.

The Side Chick Who Turned Into a Wife

The Side Chick Who Turned Into a Wife

CPSIA information can be obtained
at www.ICGtesting.com
Printed in the USA
LVOW10s1918180917
549133LV00015B/1118/P